SNOW IS NOT THE TIME

ALASKA COZY MYSTERY #4

WENDY MEADOWS

MAJESTIC OWL PUBLISHING LLC

CHAPTER ONE

Conrad knocked on the back door of Sarah's cabin as a hard wind rocked him back on his heels. As he waited for Sarah to answer the door, his eyes studied the snow-covered landscape. "So peaceful," he said in a low voice. Winds howled through trees dripping with ice and dusted with snow. The trees swayed back and forth in the dream-like snowscape. The trees, Conrad thought, surveying the white world with watery eyes, seemed to be waving at the cold, gray sky looming over the cabin. "No creepy snowmen...no mafia...no lousy British intelligence agent...everything at peace..."

He heard the back door open. "Conrad?"

"Hey," he said, turning to look into a pair of beautiful, intelligent eyes. "Mind if I come in, Sarah?"

Sarah glanced down at the pink robe she had pulled on

after a relaxing hot shower. The hour was early and she was busy working on her next novel. But the expression lurking on Conrad's face told her something was wrong. "Please, not another murder," she begged, feeling the cold winds reaching for her through the open door.

Conrad shook his head with a smile. "Not here in Snow Falls. Not even a traffic ticket," he reassured her. Pulling up the collar of his black coat, he lowered his head against the wind. "Really cold out here, Sarah."

"Oh, sure, come inside," Sarah said quickly. She backed away from the door and stepped into the kitchen. The room smelled of fresh coffee and hot, freshly baked muffins. "I was writing."

Conrad stepped into the kitchen and closed the back door. As he kicked snow off his boots, he drew in a deep, appreciative breath. "And baking," he added. "I could use some of whatever you baked. And you know how much I love your coffee."

Sarah nodded her head at the kitchen table, suppressing a smile. "Sit down," she told him.

Conrad sat down at his usual spot and watched Sarah walk over to the kitchen counter and take a muffin from the batch that sat cooling on the top of the stove. She placed the muffin on a white plate and then filled a brown mug full of hot coffee. "Blueberry muffins," she announced, carrying it over to the table.

Conrad took the plate and mug with grateful hands. "Thanks, Sarah. I'm a bit late getting started this morning. I was up most of the night talking with a friend in New York."

Sarah sat down across from Conrad and decided to let the man have a few breaths before interrogating him. "It's been quiet these last couple of weeks. I'm not complaining, either. For a while, I felt like I was living back in Los Angeles." She shook her head wordlessly.

"Yeah, it got crazy there for a while," Conrad admitted. He picked up the still-warm muffin and took a bite. "Feels like we got caught up in a stampede. I think we did okay, though."

Sarah nodded her head. "I still expect to see a snowman waiting for me every time I pull into my driveway," she confessed. "But behind every creepy snowman is a human being—a human who's monstrous on the inside."

Conrad took another bite of his muffin. "Yeah," he said. He was silent, reflecting. "Amanda has been great through it all."

"June Bug has been incredible," Sarah beamed, as she thought proudly of her best friend. "I don't know where I'd be if Amanda hadn't stood by me. Well...I do know; I would be dead."

"Yep," Conrad agreed, "Amanda sure saved our butts a

time or two. She's something special. You both are, Sarah. I'm impressed."

"Don't be impressed by our bravery and spur-of-the-moment thinking," Sarah replied. "Whenever I took a case in Los Angeles, I gathered evidence, analyzed, questioned suspects, formulated theories and opinions, followed up on leads, followed my gut, consulted forensic experts, the works. Maybe all that training has helped me, but the last three cases we worked on I shot from my hip most of the time, just hoping to hit my target."

Conrad took a sip of coffee. "I know what you mean," he agreed. "We've been running against the wind lately, to say the least."

"You can say that again," Sarah said, nodding her head toward the outside world through her back door. "People are nuts out there, Conrad, and their insanity doesn't stop at the Alaska state line. Even in small towns like this, we have to deal with the criminally insane. Maybe not as much as they would have to in Los Angeles or New York, but a dose of bad medicine always manages to creep into small places."

Conrad stared at the back door, musing on the stormy scene outside. "We were lucky last time, Sarah. We had two teenage troublemakers show up who turned out to be a blessing in disguise, helping us distract Bradley at a crucial moment. It was a gamble and a lot could have gone wrong. I didn't expect the female agent to eliminate

Bradley's two men, either. Her actions alone saved our butts. I was preparing to dig in for a firefight. The tide turned in our favor...but we both know the tide could have just as easily turned red."

"I know," Sarah acknowledged, reaching for her own cup of coffee and wrapping her fingers around its warmth. "Sometimes I still wonder what would have happened in the case before that if Amanda hadn't shown up and slugged that psycho model in the face when she did. And what about the mafia?"

Conrad looked at Sarah, shaking his head in amazement. "You saved my butt that time."

"But Amanda saved me," Sarah pointed out with a fond smile. "And that's the way it is, isn't it? When the unknown rears its ugly head, we human beings jump into a dark hole and start feeling our way around, hoping to find a way out before the darkness swallows us whole. And somewhere in the darkness—sometimes—a friend or two jumps in and saves you."

Conrad took another sip of coffee. They both sat in silence and listened to the wind howl outside. At least it wasn't snowing, Conrad thought. "Sarah...speaking of jumping into a dark hole, I've been talking to a friend in New York."

Sarah leaned back in her chair and slowly folded her arms. "It's a good thing I decided to get in some writing time instead of opening my coffee shop today. Not that any of the locals will complain about me not opening my shop. Maybe my coffee isn't the greatest. But," she said with a smile slowly returning to her pretty face, "my cinnamon rolls are."

"I love your coffee," Conrad assured her, then felt surprised that he had used the word love. "You make good, strong coffee. That's what people need. I don't care for all the jazz people fill their coffee cups with today. My grandfather drank his coffee strong and black, and so do I."

Sarah smiled at Conrad even though her gut was waiting for him to spill bad news into her lap. "Thank you for the compliment, Conrad." She liked hearing this from him. "It means a lot, coming from you."

Conrad stared into Sarah's eyes. He wanted nothing more than to forget about the business at hand and ask this beautiful woman out to lunch. The skies were cold, icy, and gray, but the roads were clear. He knew the diner in town would be open and serving delicious food. It would be nice to sit with Sarah and talk with her over coffee and apple pie. It would be nice to hear her laugh and see her smile. It would be nice to take her hand and walk down to her coffee shop and watch her bake cinnamon rolls. Something in him ached at the thought of all this, just within reach. Instead, he had to ask for help. He looked away from her eyes briefly and gazed out at the snow again. "A friend of mine was killed."

Sarah nodded and felt her smile slip away. "In New York?"

"In Minnesota," Conrad answered. "In a town called Winneshabba, about an hour north of Saint Cloud." He took another sip of coffee and then said hopefully, "Up for another road trip, Detective Garland?"

Sarah knew that she needed at least six to eight months of serious writing time in order to complete her latest novel. Every second counted. And not only did she not have the time to write the way she needed, but she barely had time to open her coffee shop, which bothered her.

And yet, there was also the prospect of a road trip with Conrad and another case to work on. She tried to tell herself she was most excited about the case, but what also warmed her was the idea of spending time with this man who she had come to care for, perhaps more deeply than she realized.

"Conrad, I'm torn..." she started to say. "I'm really behind schedule on my latest book and I don't want to put my deadline on your investigation."

Conrad heard the strain in her voice. "I understand," he said, trying not to sound disappointed.

But the instant she saw the look on his face, Sarah felt her heart twinge. She tried to cover her tracks by switching back into investigative mode. "Who was your friend that was murdered?" she asked.

"Mickey Slate," Conrad replied.

"Was that his real name?"

Conrad nodded his head. "Mickey and I grew up together. Mickey," Conrad said in a tired voice, "Mickey had a tough old man who liked the bottle, you know? The kid became familiar with a hard fist before he was even five years old. Sometimes he'd show up at school with a split lip or black eye or some bruised ribs. But hey, it was Brooklyn, and no one said jack. You learned the hard way that opening your mouth and getting involved in someone else's business meant bad news for you." Conrad reached into his jacket pocket and took out a battered photo of his friend, evidently from a number of years ago. Sarah could see the toughness written on Mickey Slate's face in the picture.

"I understand," Sarah said.

"Do you?" Conrad looked into Sarah's eyes. "Yeah, I guess you do."

"Keep talking," Sarah pressed.

Conrad sipped on his coffee. "Mickey was always getting into fights as he grew up. In high school, he joined a gang called the Back Alley Blades...a deadly bunch of greasers."

"Greasers?"

Conrad nodded. "Don't let the term fool you. We're not talking about a bunch of guys singing in a musical, here. We're talking about guys who carried switch blades, guns, pipes, chains, broken bottles, anything they could get their hands on, to a fight. We're talking about guys who chewed pain like it was candy and ate punches for breakfast." Conrad put down his coffee. "One time, I watched the Blades go toe to toe with another gang, the Red Widow Killers."

"Colorful names."

"The Red Widow Killers were lethal. Those boys ruled the streets of Brooklyn. The street cops at that time didn't dare say a word to them...nobody did."

"Except the Back Alley Blades?"

Conrad nodded again. "The Blades and the Killers went at each other like two vicious pit bulls." He closed his eyes. "I was seventeen at the time, in my senior year of high school. By that time, I thought I had seen some pretty bad stuff go down in my life...I was wrong. By the time the fight was over, there were fourteen dead bodies lying in the street. The guys who didn't get killed had been beaten or stabbed or shot too badly to even walk...a bunch of kids filled with rage."

In her mind, Sarah imagined the brawl taking place. She saw two gangs prowling down a dirty, wet alley yelling threats at each other, surrounded by run-down buildings and rusted cars. She saw the members of each gang brandishing weapons that gleamed in the darkness, sharp and deadly. And then she saw the gangs clash. The picture of it made her shudder with fear.

"Did your friend's gang walk away victorious?" she asked.

"That's right. The Blades were outnumbered that morning, but when the fight cleared, more Blades were standing than Killers."

"I see." Sarah realized Conrad was telling her about this gang fight for a reason. "So your friend Mickey was a pretty tough guy."

"Tough isn't the word," Conrad said. "Mickey didn't like anyone, not even the guys in his gang. But he and I grew up in the same building, and we were buddies from when we were about five years old."

Sarah studied Conrad's eyes. The truth hit her and she drew in a sharp breath. "The only person Mickey liked in his gang was you, then, right?"

Conrad took a bite of his muffin and wouldn't meet her eyes for a long moment, lost in thought. "I regret being a member of the Blades, Sarah. I regret...what I was back then. I regret what Mickey and I both were."

"Is that why you became a cop?"

"Let's just say that I wanted to make amends for all the damage I caused." Conrad paused. "Good muffin."

"Thanks."

Conrad took his last bite of muffin. "Mickey wouldn't have gone down without a fight," he stated, staring out the kitchen window as the wind picked up outside. "And Mickey wasn't the type of guy to ever ask for help, even from me. On the day when we tangled with the Killers, he was stabbed twice in the gut and beaten pretty badly. But he walked all the way to the hospital by himself."

"That sounds more like stupidity than bravery," Sarah said doubtfully. "I understand what you mean, though."

"At the time, I was impressed. The hospital was miles away."

In her mind, Sarah watched a wounded kid struggling down one dirty block after another, holding his stomach, determined to remain tough to the end.

Sarah rose to get herself another cup of coffee. She had a feeling it was going to be a very long day. "What did Mickey do for a living?"

Conrad finished off his coffee. "You'd never believe it, but that tough kid grew up to became a corporate lawyer. The guy had brains as well as guts."

Sarah poured coffee into her green mug and brought the coffee pot back to the kitchen table and refilled Conrad's mug. "Who did he work for?"

"McCallister Security."

"I've heard of them. McCallister has offices scattered all the way from the East Coast to the West Coast. The McCallister family is pretty rich and successful, I gather."

"McCallister is the second biggest security firm in America," Conrad said. "Anderson and Stewart are the biggest, apparently."

"When I was living in Los Angeles, I heard rumors that Anderson and Stewart were considering selling out to McCallister," Sarah replied. "I wonder whatever happened with that? Well, what kind of security do they do, exactly?"

"McCallister deals with everything from overseas private security operations to small town bank guards. McCallister makes the National Security Agency look like small potatoes."

Sarah gave Conrad a strange look. "The NSA is an agency of the Department of Defense run by politicians whose only intentions are to control info while violating the privacy of American citizens," she retorted drily.

Conrad was surprised to hear Sarah talk like a crazed

conspiracy theorist. "Next you're going to tell me the CIA created Facebook to monitor people's lives?"

"People post their personal information and photos all the time. They update their status about what they're doing, might do, have done. Facebook and Twitter are a dream come true for the CIA, FBI, Department of Homeland Security, the IRS, and all the rest of those agencies that have to take a peek every now and then..." Sarah trailed off as she focused on Conrad's eyes, which were twinkling mischievously. "Very funny, Conrad. I'm serious," she protested.

"Hey, I'm right on board with you," Conrad promised. "The American people are controlled and manipulated through a social engineering program that is allowing politicians to become richer and richer while they gain more and more power and the American public loses more and more of its freedoms. But we're cops, and our duty is to chase down the bad guys."

Sarah sighed. "Too bad we can't get all the bad guys," she said. "Okay, so forget about my personal feelings toward the NSA. We know Mickey worked for McCallister. That means it's possible he was killed over something he knew."

"Yep."

Sarah sipped her coffee. "Mickey was killed in Minnesota, right?"

"Uh-huh."

"But you said you spoke to someone in New York?" Sarah asked, confused.

"That's the thing. Before he died, Mickey called me from New York," Conrad explained. "My friend back in New York later told me that someone took a few shots at Mickey the day he called me. Mickey slipped through the bullets and ended up in Minnesota somehow. That's where he died."

"I see," Sarah said. "This friend of yours knows Mickey personally?"

Conrad sighed. "No. My friend once belonged to the Killers, the gang we tangled with in our earlier days. He never forgave Mickey for putting his brother in a wheelchair. It's a long story, okay?"

"I bet it is," Sarah said, shaking her head with a sigh. "People never cease to amaze me. So how did your ex-Killers friend know what had happened to Mickey?"

Conrad started to reply when suddenly the back door opened and Amanda burst into the kitchen, covered from head to toe in an icy sprinkling of snow. "Here I am," she announced happily.

Sarah gave Amanda a confused look as Amanda stomped snow from her feet and began to remove her white coat. "Here you are?" she repeated.

"Sure." Amanda smiled as she hung up her coat. "Our movie date, love, remember?"

Conrad watched Amanda remove the pink ski cap from her head and then take off a pair of thick pink gloves. He chuckled. "Cute sweater."

Amanda glanced down at the oversized knitted pink sweater she was wearing and tapped the white bunny that was appliqued on the front. "On cold days like today, Mr. Bunny and I prefer warmth over style. And speaking of warmth, my it's cozy in here. Did I...interrupt something?" Amanda teased, tousling her hair to shake out the icy crystals.

"What? Ah—no..." Conrad said, standing up a touch too fast. He could feel Sarah's eyes on him and that only increased the uncomfortable warmth of his face. "I...a friend of mine was killed. I came here to ask Sarah for her help."

Amanda immediately frowned. "How many people can die in one small town?" she said in an incredulous voice. "Please, can't we just go back to fussing over some spilled tea like we were a couple of weeks ago?"

"Not here, June Bug. No one was murdered in Snow Falls," Sarah assured her. "Conrad's friend was killed in Minnesota."

"Well, thank goodness for that," Amanda said and then clapped her hands over her mouth. "Oh, Conrad, I'm sorry. I didn't mean to say it like that. I'm so sorry about your friend."

"I understand," Conrad said. "I feel the same way." He ran a hand over his face in sudden fatigue.

Amanda walked over to the kitchen table, grabbed Sarah's half-full mug and took a sip. "Forgot about our movie date, didn't you, Los Angeles?"

"Sorry," Sarah winced. "I woke up early and started writing. I only took a little break to bake some muffins and then went back to work."

"Muffins?"

Conrad tossed a thumb at the kitchen counter. "Blueberry muffins. And they're well worth a skipped movie."

Amanda hurried over to the counter and tore into a muffin. "Delicious. Your coffee may be a bit strong, but your baking skills are amazing."

"Maybe I should open a bakery instead," Sarah rolled her eyes. "If you two will excuse me, I think I'll go change into something more appropriate."

"We'll be here," Amanda promised.

Conrad watched her walk out of the kitchen. He found it impossible to look away from Sarah's beauty. Amanda noticed the look in Conrad's eyes. She sat down in

Sarah's chair and cleared her throat. Conrad looked at her, startled. "What?"

"You know what," Amanda grinned. "So, when is the wedding?"

"What? No, no. Sarah and I are friends, Amanda," Conrad protested.

"Sure, you are." Amanda smiled and sipped at her coffee. "You might be in denial, but even a blind person could see the way you two look at each other."

"You're crazy," Conrad exclaimed. He cautiously sat back down. "Believe it or not, I have other things on my mind besides romance. I have to fly to Minnesota and investigate my friend's death. I was hoping Sarah might tag along with me...and you, as well. It seems like we three make a good team."

Amanda studied Conrad's face, thinking. "My Jack came home for one week and then returned to London. I'll be alone for the next two weeks, but that doesn't mean I want to spend those two weeks chasing after a bunch of alley cats crazier than my Aunt Jean was."

"I understand," Conrad said. He knew how both Sarah and Amanda felt. Sarah was retired, and Amanda had her husband to think about. Who was he to drag them into a dangerous case of murder again?

And, he thought, did Sarah not feel what he had felt

during their last investigation? Was he imagining that electric charge that passed between them when they were on the trail of a murderer? It was more than just the thrill of the chase – unless it wasn't.

Amanda looked at Conrad. "Oh, don't make that sad puppy dog face at me," she smiled, rolling her eyes fondly.

"What sad puppy dog face?"

"*That* sad puppy dog face." Amanda pointed at Conrad's face and imitated his dejected, hangdog look.

Conrad raised a hand to touch his face with an impish grin. "I wasn't aware that I was a dog."

"Well, you are." Amanda sighed. "So...is Sarah going to Minnesota with you?"

"No."

"Well...I guess that leaves me," Amanda said. "I must be crazy. But how can I let you go alone with a face like that?"

Conrad felt a smile on his lips. "Thanks, Amanda. You're something else."

"I wish my husband knew that. It seems that taking care of his dad is more important than taking care of his wife, at the moment."

"I'm sure that's not true. When we had dinner at your

cabin last week while Jack was here, the man couldn't take his eyes off you."

Amanda put her left hand under her chin and sighed. "Then why is he back in London?"

"Because, as a son, he has a certain duty toward his old man," Conrad reminded her gently. "The heart may be torn, Amanda, but the heart never forgets who it loves."

"So now you're a poet," Amanda joked. "But seriously, thanks for cheering me up. Now, fill me in. What were you and Sarah talking about?"

Conrad drew in a deep breath and went through the details. He finished with his friend Mickey being found dead in a motel room in Minnesota. "That's all I have for now."

"I'm still in shock that you were a gang member," Amanda said, shaking her head in amazement. "I could slap you silly. You silly bloke."

"My time with the Blades was a long time ago."

"Let's hope it stays that way," Sarah said, walking into the kitchen.

Amanda looked at Sarah and tutted, "Ladies and gentlemen, here we have a beautiful woman wearing a plain brown dress with her hair in a plain ponytail. Yes, Sarah Garland is ready to dazzle the world."

"This dress is warm," Sarah protested.

Amanda shifted her eyes meaningfully toward Conrad. She said in an undertone, "You have other dresses."

Flustered, Sarah smoothed her skirt. "This dress is fine for today," she said. She poured herself another cup of coffee. "Conrad?"

"Yes?"

"Buy two extra plane tickets. Amanda and I are flying to Minnesota with you." Sarah locked eyes with Amanda. "I know you, June Bug. By now you've agreed to team up with Conrad again."

"I sure did," Amanda smiled impishly. "How else was I going to get you to follow me?"

Conrad stood up from the kitchen table, clearing his throat nervously. His smile threatened to redden his face again, so he ducked his head. "I...uh, already booked our flight," he explained with a sheepish smile, easing toward the back door. "Our plane leaves Anchorage at ten o'clock sharp tomorrow morning. You ladies had better pack. We'll be staying in Minnesota for a week, maybe more."

Sarah propped her hands onto her hips. "So you knew I would agree to tag along?"

"I hoped," Conrad confessed, opening the back door. "I'll be by early to pick you ladies up. Be ready."

Amanda watched Conrad hurry out the back door and close it behind him. "We're crazy," she told Sarah. "Our lives just returned to a peaceful state, and here we are chasing after danger again."

"In Minnesota, no less," Sarah added, plopping down in the chair Conrad had just vacated. She couldn't help but feel that behind her indignation at Conrad's little ploy, she felt a thrill. "I have to get my book written, June Bug. I'm way behind. But...the truth is...I have a little writer's block."

"I know you do."

"How?" Sarah asked, confused.

"Your eyes were really wandering when you had dinner with me and Jack last week. I could tell what you were thinking about," Amanda explained. "But seriously, Los Angeles, who can blame you? Your mind must feel like mush right about now."

"I admit, my brain does feel like it's been strapped into a straitjacket and thrown into a padded room."

"You need a rest," Amanda pointed out. "Unfortunately, we're two crazy ladies who seem to thrive on danger. So for now, strap into that straitjacket again because we have another case to solve."

"And you, of all people, seem excited about it," Sarah added with a smile.

21

"Well," Amanda said in a strange voice, "I have to admit that after we dealt with Bradley and his loony gang, I realized that what we do is important...and a bit exciting. Bradley was attempting to release a virus that could have killed millions, and we stopped him. I don't mean to sound insane, but...I was scared out of my wits, but now that we're sitting here alive and I can review everything with a clear mind, well, the things we've been through together have been...thrilling."

"Dealing with a crazy model, a deranged mafia wise guy, and a deadly British agent was thrilling?"

"Absolutely." Amanda smiled and raised her coffee into the air. "Cheers, love."

"I must be out of my mind," Sarah groaned good-naturedly as she raised her coffee mug into the air too. "Hey, did Conrad tell you that his friend who was murdered worked for McCallister?"

"Yes." Amanda took a sip of coffee. "McCallister is the second largest security firm in America with local and global offices," she recited in a precise tone. "I have been informed, Los Angeles, and I'm up to date."

"And you're not the least bit concerned that Jason McCallister's people, the ones who probably killed Conrad's friend, might decide to follow the same protocol regarding certain investigators who might get too close and uncover the truth?"

"The thought did cross my mind," Amanda admitted, "but we don't really know if Mr. McCallister killed poor Mickey. All we know is that Mickey worked for McCallister as one of their numerous law blokes."

"The ball seems to be in McCallister's court, though." Sarah stood up. "Want another muffin?"

"Please."

Sarah fetched two muffins and returned to the kitchen table. She handed one to Amanda and sat down. "Conrad said that the first attempt on his friend's life took place in New York."

"Which," Amanda said in a thoughtful voice, "ran the poor man out of town."

"But why Minnesota?" Sarah asked, nibbling on her muffin. "Why did this Mickey guy run to a small town in Minnesota?"

"That's what we have to investigate," Amanda replied and took a large bite of her muffin. "Delicious, love. Your baking skills are amazing."

"I wish my coffee skills were just as amazing," Sarah sighed. "At least Conrad likes my coffee."

"I bet he does," Amanda grinned.

"Don't start," Sarah begged. "Conrad and I are only

friends. I'm not ready to accept an invitation to dinner, let alone entertain the idea of romance."

"I know, I know," Amanda said warmly, "but please, love, don't slam the door in Conrad's face."

"Right now," Sarah pointed out, "I'm more interested in working on my novel. You know being a writer is very important to me. I'm passionate about my work, and I love writing my stories."

"Your last story nearly cost you everything," Amanda said in a worried voice. "Seriously, Los Angeles, why can't you write about fluffy clouds and sunshine?"

"Because," Sarah countered quickly, "all I know is dark alleys and dark minds. Every writer writes about what they know. I spent years delving into the minds of killers in order to capture them. I explore my experiences...and transform them into stories."

"You're a sick woman. You're very good at changing the subject, don't think I didn't notice that, but you're also sick," Amanda grinned. She polished off her muffin. "But we're all sick in one way or another. I, for instance, used pickle-green nail polish on my toes last week. How sick is that? And before you agree, let me just point out that I was in a mood, okay?"

"You were sitting in your bedroom, angry at Jack, listening to your jazz records, eating chocolate and

24

drinking fruit punch," Sarah guessed and winked at her friend. "Did I hit a home run?"

Amanda wrinkled her nose at Sarah. "Yes, Detective Garland, you have once again penetrated the mind of a very sick criminal and captured her most deranged character traits with your splendid mystery-solving skills."

"June Bug," Sarah laughed, "it would take me many lifetimes to capture all of your character traits. I'm still aghast at how you eat pickles with marshmallows."

"My demented mind will never reveal the reason." Amanda let out a spooky mad scientist laugh. "Now, please, go into the basement and fetch my second head. Two heads are better than one, after all."

"I wish I had two heads. Maybe an extra brain would have an idea to break through this writer's block. Then I'd leave that one at home to write and send the second head to Minnesota." Sarah knew if she stayed home she would only write and rewrite the same sentence over and over again, as she had been doing for most of the early morning. "By the way, it's kinda early for a movie date, isn't it?"

Amanda grinned. "We didn't have a movie date planned, love," she confessed. "I was lonely and needed an excuse to come over. I knew you would think you forgot if I mentioned it."

Sarah stared at Amanda. Behind the grin she saw loneliness in her best friend's eyes. "Honey, you can come over and stay with me anytime you want. You don't need to make up an excuse."

"I was hoping you'd say that, I actually have my suitcase in my truck," Amanda beamed. "I love my home, but it's sad being there alone. I thought I would stay with you and do girly stuff until Jack returns home. Now it seems that we're about to take off on another exciting case." Amanda plopped her chin down onto her hands. "Can you believe Mr. New York actually fought in a gang?"

Sarah leaned back in her chair. "June Bug," she said, "at this point, anything is possible. Not only do I believe that Conrad was a member of the Back Alley Blades, but I believe that someone from his old neighborhood might have been involved in the killing of his friend Mickey."

Amanda nodded her head but remained quiet. Outside, a light snow began to fall.

CHAPTER TWO

Sarah pulled back the dark green curtain and peered out into the wet, rainy parking lot. "I don't know what's worse...snow or freezing cold rain," she said to Amanda in a depressed voice.

Amanda shrugged her shoulders and opened her light brown suitcase. "In London, you become best mates with cold rain. I don't mind."

"Well, I like warm rain," Sarah replied, still focused on the rainy parking lot. Its cracked paving was attached to the Snowflake Inn, a single-story motel with worn, green wooden siding. It held fifteen rundown rooms with five rooms to a wing. The first wing ran parallel to the street while the second and third wings ran perpendicular. A large wooden snowflake sign stood above the motel lobby that looked like it hadn't been updated since the 1960s. Tall weeds poked out of banks of dirty, half-melted snow, and trash littered the parking lot. "How picturesque," Sarah commented.

"This is where Mickey bit the bullet," Amanda reminded Sarah as she began to unpack. Glancing around the room, she grimaced at the sight of the worn, brown shag carpet, with numerous cigarette burns and mysterious stains. Her eyes fell on the two queen beds with their two miserable, ugly brown blankets. "I'm no spoiled princess, but this place is enough to make a person run to a shrink. The walls," Amanda said with a shudder, "are right out of a horror movie."

Sarah turned away from the window and looked at the badly stained walls. "The walls look like someone lost their lunch on them," she said in a disgusted voice. "Amanda, I can't sleep here. I'm going to get a room at a chain hotel out by the interstate."

Amanda stopped in the middle of unpacking a gray sweater. She shook her head in defeat. "Grab your suitcase, love," she said and threw the sweater back into her own suitcase. "No need to tell me twice."

Sarah retrieved her suitcase, hurried to the door, and yanked it open, only to be greeted by Conrad. "Going someplace?" he asked. He held a black umbrella over his head.

"Yes," Sarah said firmly, "Amanda and I are going to get a decent room."

Conrad nodded with an apologetic smile. "I was thinking the same," he confessed. "I won't stand in your way," Conrad continued, gesturing with a thumb to the depressing parking lot over his shoulder and the winding road back to the interstate.

Sarah felt relief wash through her. She grabbed her own umbrella and fussed with her white coat collar with her free hand. "This motel ought to be condemned."

Amanda set down her suitcase and began to button up her pink coat. "I agree."

"Back in the late sixties, this motel was owned by a hippie who was into the 'Peace and Love' movement, which meant this whole place was a stomping ground for drug users and drunks."

"Kill your brain and destroy your liver...yeah, that's far out, man," Amanda said in a sour voice.

"The owner looks like he never left the old days; when we checked in, he still looked pretty 'far out,'" Sarah said, rolling her eyes. "Conrad, I didn't question Mr. Dean. I can't say I want to go back into the front lobby and talk to him, either. The lobby smells of urine and cigarette smoke. Did you get anything out of him?"

"Dean was paid to keep his mouth shut and he's doing just that," Conrad said in a calm tone. "You could toss the guy on the grill for weeks and all you would get out of him would be a request for a cigarette."

"Let's go, then," Sarah said. She stepped out into the rain. Amanda followed close behind and hurried under the umbrella as soon as Sarah popped it open.

As Sarah walked to their gray rental SUV, a black Lincoln Town Car pulled into the parking lot. Conrad slowly eased his right hand into his black leather jacket, found his gun, and waited. Sarah transferred the umbrella in her hand to Amanda and watched the black car creep past the gray SUV, turn around, then hang a right onto the front street and drive away. "No license plate," she commented to Conrad.

Conrad removed his right hand from his pocket. "I saw," he said grimly. He nodded his head toward the SUV. "Get in, ladies."

Amanda jogged to the rear right passenger's side door, pulled it open, tossed in her suitcase, closed the umbrella, and planted herself firmly into her seat. "Hand me your suitcase," she told Sarah quickly. Sarah complied and jumped into the front passenger's seat. Conrad ran around to the driver's side door, yanked it open, hopped into his seat, and buckled up. "Let's move," he said, "and see where that black Lincoln wants to meet."

"Meet?" Amanda asked.

"That Lincoln wasn't just coming by to take a look," Sarah explained as Conrad backed up, then sped out onto the street and peeled right. "That was an invitation to follow." Sarah looked out of the passenger's window at the rainy trees standing beside the road like sad, forgotten members of a lost platoon. Driveways marked by rusted mailboxes flashed past as Conrad sped up. The driveways, Sarah saw, led to dilapidated homes that matched the motel in style and condition. Rundown cars and trucks were parked in the driveways, choked with overgrown weeds. "What a sad place," she remarked.

"Every town has its lower end," Conrad said. He spotted the taillights of the black Lincoln ahead. "I'm sure the Lincoln is going to take us to a very nice part of Winneshabba."

Amanda pushed her suitcase into the cargo space of the SUV and then Sarah's too, as excitement rushed through her veins. Maybe she was insane to be excited, she thought, but she couldn't help it. After successfully dealing with three vicious killers back in Alaska, she felt hungry to take on the world. "Don't lose the car," she urged Conrad.

Conrad glanced at Amanda in the rearview mirror. "Yes, ma'am," he said and then aimed a glance at Sarah. "I think we've created a female Sherlock Holmes."

Sarah chuckled in response as she subtly leaned forward to check the gun holstered at her right ankle. She felt like she was back in Los Angeles, driving to the scene of a homicide. But she was with Conrad now, of course, and the feeling was intense—and secure. Back in Alaska, their cases had made her feel imprisoned somehow, trapped in the little town and unable to utilize the full scope of her skills. Possibly because, she thought, each case had exploded in her face without warning, forcing her to become a rat trapped in a deadly maze. But now, the SUV raced past the muddy driveways and wet trees of Winneshabba and, as the windshield wipers fought the rain on the windshield, she felt the familiar feeling of cop work in her gut—a certain sense of control and stability that she lacked in Snow Falls.

"Nobody else knew we were in town," she commented to Conrad. "I bet Mr. Dean at the motel made a phone call to whoever paid him off."

"Yep," Conrad said, still carefully following the black Lincoln.

Sarah settled back in her seat. As she did, the memory of the disturbed model who had tortured her with hideous snowmen crawled into her mind. The model hissed at Sarah and pointed at a creepy snowman. The snowman was standing in Sarah's writing den, wearing a black leather jacket and chewing on a peppermint candy cane. It was laughing insanely. Then the snowman walked over to Sarah's writing desk, sat down, and began writing something. Sarah closed her eyes and tried to shake the image from her mind.

"Are you okay, Los Angeles?" Amanda asked, sensing something was the matter with her best friend.

"I'm okay," Sarah promised and opened her eyes. "I...bad memory, that's all," she said, running her hand through her hair. The image of the creepy snowman sitting at her writing desk began to slowly fade away. "Sometimes I wish I could walk into a cozy shop, browse around, buy some delicious fudge, and then spend the rest of my day sipping coffee in a warm café cuddled up with a good book."

Conrad glanced at Sarah. In her demeanor, he saw the working mind of a tough, brilliant cop. In her eyes, he saw a beautiful woman yearning to forget her past and embrace a warm future where she could soak in the sun. He knew that Sarah was a prisoner to the darkness she had dared to walk in for so many years and that she would never be able to escape her past—not completely, anyway.

"I can turn around," he offered, troubled by her look.

"What good would that do?" Sarah asked. Focusing her eyes on the taillights of the black Lincoln, she cleared her mind. "The Lincoln has no license plate, which means the law in this town must be bought."

"Agreed," Conrad said.

"Somebody fill me in, please," Amanda begged.

"Would you drive around without a license plate?" Sarah asked.

"No...I mean, if I did, I would chance getting pulled over, having my truck impounded and—" Amanda stopped. "Oh, I see."

Conrad slowed the SUV down as the black Lincoln ahead of them halted briefly at a four-way stop, and then turned right, toward the small downtown district. Conrad cautiously followed at a safe distance. "I can't get a coroner's report in this case," he said. "Not from Alaska, anyway. Maybe if I speak to the coroner here personally, I might be able to get a few answers."

As they approached the downtown area, Sarah watched the landscape transform from poor and rundown into prosperous and clean. Lushly landscaped yards surrounded by well-kept two-story homes sitting at the end of expensive-looking cobblestone driveways began to appear. She saw everything from BMWs to fancy sports cars to expensive SUVs sitting in the driveways. "The mind is such..." she mused.

"What's that?" Conrad asked.

"The mind," Sarah explained. "Some people have mansion minds, some people have two-story home minds, some people have ranch-style home minds, and some people have trailer park minds. How a person keeps his home, his yard, his car...it's like seeing into that person's mind. Of course," she continued, coming out of her reverie, "many good men live in poor homes and a killer can live in a mansion."

"You make a good point. After all," said Conrad as he looked over at Sarah and then focused back on the rainy road, "we are tailing a brand spanking new Lincoln, and do you think the driver will turn out to be a Boy Scout?" Amanda leaned forward and waited for Sarah to respond.

"No," Sarah answered honestly, "far from it. I would bet my cabin that they've been sent to sweet talk our ears off and follow up with personal threats if we refuse to take the candy."

Amanda leaned back in her seat, nibbling one fingernail. "I guess there's only one way to find out," she said with apprehension.

Soon enough, the Lincoln cruised into the downtown district of Winneshabba and parked in front of a tea house. The street was lined with two-story buildings in distinguished red brick and Queen Anne style wooden edifices, all neatly kept and enticing to the eye. More of those expensive-looking vehicles were parked here and there in front of the buildings. Sarah studied the street with a trained eye. Though she longed to go for a stroll and find the perfect spot to wait out the dreary afternoon, she tried to memorize the street in case it was important later. She saw an art studio, a candy shop, a bakery, a computer store, a toy store, a bookstore and an inviting diner situated between a lawyer's office and a real estate office. "Do I stay in the SUV or come with you?" Amanda asked, her voice jumpy.

"You'd better come inside with us," Conrad said, parking next to a shiny, expensive-looking red truck.

Sarah rechecked her gun, unbuckled her seatbelt, and looked through the rain-streaked windshield one more time. The Lincoln was parked on the opposite side of the red truck. "Ready?"

"Ready," Conrad said and grabbed his umbrella. He opened the driver's door and cautiously stepped out onto the wet ground. Amanda got out of the SUV, opened her umbrella, and waited for Sarah to join her. "Tea, love?" she asked.

Sarah stepped under the umbrella and nodded her head. "Why not?"

"Careful now," Conrad said, spotting a man wearing a black suit entering the tea house. "Stay close."

Amanda took Sarah's hand. "I'm close."

"We're a team," Sarah assured her. "Last time we worked solo we almost lost touch...for good."

Amanda squeezed Sarah's hand. "Never again, love."

"Okay, the Hallmark card moment is over, ladies," Conrad said. "Let's go."

Sarah and Amanda followed Conrad to the glass entrance door of the tea shop and paused. Conrad glanced over his shoulder at the Lincoln, clenched his jaw slightly, then pulled open the glass door and stepped inside. Sarah steeled herself, then followed him into a warm, brightly lit room filled with mingled scents of jasmine, green tea, and roses. Round wooden tables with pretty white tablecloths sat on a glossy hardwood floor. Light pink wallpaper with a floral pattern covered the walls. Overhead, soft piano music floated down from speakers in the four corners of the room. The only thing missing, conspicuously, were the employees.

But the man in the dark suit stood watching them enter.

"Please, sit down," he said with extreme politeness.

Sarah watched the man take off his black jacket, drape it over a wooden chair, and sit down at a table in the middle of the room. The man had dark gray hair and a very thin face that was shrewd and calculating. In fact, he reminded her a little of the British agent, Bradley Preston. Even though the man before her looked different, physically speaking, his voice and manner were almost identical to Bradley's. Intelligent, but cold.

"We'll stand, thank you," Conrad said, taking note of the metal spiral staircase at the far right side of the room. Two men wearing gray suits were standing at the staircase. Their faces were emotionless, yet somehow conveyed an air of concealed menace.

"Very well. My name is Mr. Snyder Smith."

"Detective Spencer, Detective Garland, and—Detective

Funnel," Conrad introduced everyone. Amanda met his eyes and tried to conceal her surprised smile at being named an honorary detective on this occasion.

Snyder Smith removed a pair of driving gloves from his hands and slowly placed them down onto the table. "You are here because of one Mickey Slate, correct?" he asked.

"Could be," Conrad said, keeping Snyder's men in view from the corner of his eye, "but then again, maybe Mr. Dean is a bit paranoid and made a premature call."

Snyder didn't appear pleased with Conrad's remark. "The death of Mickey Slate was very unfortunate. As mayor of Winneshabba, I am deeply disturbed that a man committed suicide in my town."

Conrad exchanged a meaningful glance with Sarah and then looked back at Snyder. "Mickey wasn't the suicidal type, Mayor."

Snyder calmly folded his arms across his chest. "Mickey Slate was found with a rope around his neck, Detective Spencer. I'm afraid your friend was very much suicidal."

"I'd like to examine his body," Conrad replied firmly. "I know I have no jurisdiction in your town, but out of professional courtesy, I would appreciate the help."

Sarah studied Snyder's face and interjected, "Professional courtesy is always appreciated."

Snyder focused his attention on Sarah. "Is it?" he said,

sounding regretful. "Unfortunately, the body of Mickey Slate was cremated two days after his death."

Conrad's cheeks flushed with anger. "I see," he said, a muscle twitching in his jaw. "Where was the cremation done?"

"Smith's Funeral Home."

"Any relation to you, Mr. Mayor?" Conrad asked.

"Yes," he replied with a perfect poker face. "I run the funeral home, as it so happens."

Despite Sarah's immediate suspicions, she knew they couldn't afford to alienate the mayor of this small town. From the look of the two men standing by the metal staircase, it was apparent he wasn't just an ordinary mayor, either. She decided she would save some of her sharper questions for another time.

"What was Mr. Slate doing in Winneshabba?" Sarah asked, keeping her voice professional and clear.

"Of course, we can't know for certain, but it is the belief of Chief Messings and myself that the man was simply passing through. The toxicology report showed large amounts of antidepressants in his blood. Our theory is that Mr. Slate was planning to kill himself and randomly picked the Snowflake Inn as the location to do it."

"The motel is a long way off the main road," Sarah

pointed out. "And to be honest, it isn't exactly a five-star resort. Do you think that's why he chose it?"

"It's true, the Snowflake Inn has seen better days, I'm afraid," Snyder said, smoothly skipping over her question. "I'm sorry that your friend's life ended so tragically. I'm also sorry to say that there is nothing that I or anyone in Winneshabba can do to assist you in whatever it is you are searching for."

"Then why didn't you say that back at the motel?" Amanda exploded in exasperation before she could catch her tongue. She expected to receive a sharp eye from Conrad or Sarah for her outburst, but she was surprised to see that her friends supported her question and turned to Snyder for his answer.

Snyder unfolded his arms. "Bring me my tea," he called out. One of his men walked to the door at the back of the room and disappeared into the kitchen. "I'm an old-fashioned man, you might say. I like to talk in an environment that is more suitable to a civilized man," he answered Amanda.

"Well then," Amanda said with forced cheer, "no harm in that."

Sarah realized that Amanda might have shot a three-pointer from midcourt by acting simple-minded in front of Snyder. "Mr. Smith, how did you know we were at the motel?" Sarah asked even though she knew the answer.

Snyder shifted in his seat and then refolded his arms. "Detective Garland, I can understand that you must have many questions, but at the moment I cannot discuss the death of Mr. Slate in any greater detail than I already have. This is all privileged information, as I'm sure you are aware."

Conrad ignored Snyder's deflection. "Then I'm sure you won't mind if we ask some of the locals a few questions?" he asked, echoing the mayor's polite tones.

"Actually, I do," Snyder said firmly. "Detective Spencer, ours is a very quiet and safe community. The death of Mr. Slate has been kept out of the news, and as I told you, he was merely passing through. I cannot have you upsetting people with unreasonable repeated questioning. Those involved have spoken to the local authorities. And that's where the matter will remain."

"Well then," Conrad said, tossing a thumb at the front door, "I think we'll hang around and do some sightseeing for a few days...as private citizens in a free land."

Snyder narrowed his eyes. "You may remain in Winneshabba and conduct your sightseeing, Detective Spencer; however, if you disobey my order, I will certainly have you escorted out of my town."

"Sure," Conrad said. He walked to the front door and Amanda and Sarah followed. As they reached the door, Conrad stopped and turned to face Mr. Smith again.

"Mayor, let me remind you that this is a free country and that I can talk to anyone I please. Is that clear? I know my rights. If you try to bully me, then prepare for a fight. Mickey Slate was a close friend of mine and now he's dead. I want answers."

"Your friend committed suicide. There is your answer," Snyder answered, his tone acidly hostile. "If you press for a different one, then you will be met with full force. Is *that* clear, Detective Spencer?"

"I've been through worse than a tussle with a small-town mayor, Mr. Smith, and I can do it again," Conrad replied, and with that, he walked outside into the rain.

Sarah nodded her head at Amanda. "Let's go."

"Lovely place you have here," Amanda said to Snyder pleasantly, then hurried after Sarah.

Sarah found Conrad opening his umbrella outside. She stepped under the umbrella and put her hand on his shoulder. "You deliberately tested that man. Why?" she queried.

"I don't like snakes," Conrad said, "and I don't intend to be nice to one in order to be allowed to hang around town."

"We're going to be watched every second from this point forward," she protested.

"I know it was tense in there, Sarah, but you know my past...I've dealt with his type before."

Sarah bit her lip in frustration, wondering what else from Conrad's past might be lurking under the surface of this investigation.

Amanda hurried over to Sarah. "So what's the plan? I mean, we all know he wasn't telling the truth about poor Mickey."

Sarah felt like taking Conrad to task for making an enemy out of Snyder from the start. "It would have been a lot smarter to play dumb with that crook," she said in a displeased voice.

"Maybe," Conrad admitted, "but I don't like to play dumb. And I know you're smart and playing dumb isn't your favorite trick in the book, either. So, detective. What's the next move?" His eyes locked onto Sarah's with a challenge.

Sarah set her hands on her hips. The air was cold. The rain was cold. Her face was cold. Her ears were cold. The last thing her heart desired was to stand on a wet sidewalk and argue with Conrad. "We'd better make it clear that a lot of people—and I do mean a lot of people— know we're in Winneshabba."

"Why?" Amanda asked, and then she realized the answer to her own question. "Oh, I see."

"Snyder can't try anything funny if he knows too many people know we're in town," Conrad answered anyway, without looking away from Sarah. "Mickey was my friend, Sarah. We handle this case my way."

Sarah couldn't believe her ears. "We're supposed to be a team, Conrad."

Conrad looked away from the look of pleading in her eyes. "My friend was murdered and I need to know what happened. Don't ask me to play politics, okay? I don't play nice with the bad guys." He pressed his lips together to suppress the anger and sadness rising within him and turned to gaze up the street so Sarah couldn't read his face.

Sarah stepped over to Amanda's umbrella as Conrad stared through the cold, miserable rain. She was uneasy with the disagreement that had passed between them, so instead, she followed the thoughts that swirled in her mind. Wasn't Minnesota supposed to be snowy in the winter? Why in the world was it raining? And what was she doing here standing in the rain instead of back home working on her latest novel while finding the time to open her coffee shop for a measly few hours a day? "Okay, Conrad, I understand," Sarah said finally. It was as close as she could get. "Come on, drive us to a hotel. We'll grab a solid lunch and talk."

"Yeah, I'm starving," Amanda agreed. She patted Conrad

on the shoulder. "Come on, you silly bloke, you have two hungry women on your hands."

Conrad continued to stare into the distance. "Mickey had a wife and a son," he said in a low voice. "His family deserves to know the truth, Sarah. Please, let's do this case my way, okay?"

Sarah lowered her head. "Why didn't you tell me he had a wife and son? For crying out loud, that's vital information. You made it seem like Mickey Slate was a single man."

"I guess I just wasn't ready to admit to myself that I let my friend *and* his family down," Conrad said. He walked away, back towards the car.

Amanda held her umbrella over Sarah as they walked together. "This case is personal for Conrad. He needs us. And he needs you. Let's not push him away, Los Angeles, okay?"

Sarah watched Conrad position himself in the driver's seat of the SUV. "Okay," she sighed, "we'll let Conrad handle this case his way and give him all the support he needs."

Amanda patted Sarah's shoulder and opened her door at the SUV.

CHAPTER THREE

*S*nyder stood at the glass front door of the tea house and watched Amanda and Sarah climb into the SUV. He spoke into the black cell phone in his hand. "We have three problems."

"Get rid of them," a menacing voice warned him.

"I'm afraid it's not that easy, sir," Snyder said in a concerned tone. "Killing three detectives won't be as simple as killing one man. As of now, I have no idea who these three people truly are, where they're from, how many people know their location, or how many more people might be on route to Winneshabba. For now, sir, it would be very wise to let Detectives Spencer, Garland and Funnel play a few hands before we act."

"Mickey Slate is still a threat," the voice rebuked. "If

anyone finds the flash drive that contains the stolen information...well, let's just hope for your sake that never happens since you were the one in charge of retrieving it."

Snyder watched the SUV drive away into the rain with a sinking feeling. "I understand that I am at fault, Mr. M. However, it's very unlikely that the disk is even in Winneshabba. Mickey Slate drove here from New York in his personal vehicle. He could have stopped anywhere and hidden the disk. At this point in time, we have no way of knowing who he might have spoken to while he was driving. And sir, to be fair, it was your men who missed their target. Mickey Slate had the USB drive on him the morning your men shot at him."

"Snyder, I'm not interested in your theories. I'm holding you personally responsible. Is that clear? I want the drive and I want you to eliminate anyone associated with Mickey Slate," the voice hissed.

"What about the man's wife and son?"

"For the time being, leave them alone. Mickey's family will be my personal responsibility."

"I understand, sir," Snyder replied. He paused for a few seconds to steady his mind, thinking about Sarah, Amanda, and Conrad. "I'll make contact with you tomorrow at this time."

"See to it that you do," the menacing voice said and ended the call.

Snyder put away his cell phone and looked out into the rain. "Mace, Thorn, get over here," he snapped.

The two men strode up to him. "Yes, sir, Mr. Smith?"

"Follow them," Snyder ordered. "They left and drove east. Hurry."

"Yes, sir." They sprinted out into the rain, jumped into the black Lincoln, and sped away.

"Idiots," Snyder muttered. He pulled out his cell phone again and dialed the Winneshabba Chief of Police. "We need to speak in person. We have three people who just arrived in town that need to be dealt with very carefully."

A fat man with a large belly leaned forward in his black desk chair and set a half-eaten jelly donut down onto a paper napkin. "Who?" Chief Messings asked. He slowly picked up a partially-smoked cigar and began puffing on it. Knowing that stepping on the toes of a man like Snyder Smith was akin to angering a rattlesnake, Chief Messings hoped he would be able to please his boss.

"Three detectives," Mayor Snyder Smith said. "For now, I want constant surveillance on them. I've sent two of my men to locate them."

"Detectives?" Chief Messings asked. He nervously ran a hand through his thick, curly brown hair that was slowly turning gray. "Mr. Smith, I run a small police station, here. I—"

"Are you objecting to my request?" Snyder interrupted impatiently.

Chief Messings tossed his cigar back into the tin ashtray. "No, sir, Mr. Smith. I...well, I..." he fumbled and then grew silent. "Yes, sir, Mayor, I'll have my boys watch the newcomers."

"Good," Snyder snapped. "Messings, I can ruin you and will do so if you fail me. I will see to it that you spend the rest of your life in prison with all your favorite felons. Do I make myself perfectly clear?"

"Yes, sir, Mr. Smith," Chief Messings said, swallowing nervously.

"Very good. Now, let's talk about Detective Spencer, Detective Garland, and Detective Funnel."

Chief Messings's eyes widened. "Did you say Detective Garland...Detective Sarah Garland?"

"Do you know the woman?" Snyder asked.

"Do I know her?" Chief Messings repeated in a dazed voice. "Detective Sarah Garland captured the Alley Killer. Her face was plastered over every magazine and television screen across the country for a week straight."

"I see," Snyder said. He rubbed his chin. "Tell me more."

Chief Messings looked around his small office. Files and papers were piled everywhere, mingled with empty paper coffee cups and donut napkins. He despaired of locating one of the magazine articles that had featured Detective Garland.

As he cast his gaze across the mess, a polished wooden picture frame amid the clutter caught his eye. The picture frame displayed the image of his wife, a pretty, rather matronly woman holding a little schnauzer dog. She was, Chief Messings knew, at this moment preparing a lunch at home which she would bring by the office in less than an hour. "Mr. Smith," he said in a worried voice, "sir...Detective Garland is a well-known person in the law enforcement world. The last I heard she retired and moved away someplace. Why in the world is she in Winneshabba?"

"Mickey Slate is why," Snyder said. "It seems he's causing us more problems dead than alive."

"I told you to leave the man be," Chief Messings said, and then grew pale. "Mr. Mayor, sir, I didn't mean to...what I mean is...I'm sorry, sir. I was out of line. I—"

"Shut up. You were actually right, you bumbling idiot. I should have left Mickey Slate alive...for the time being. I have a mess on my hands." Snyder sighed. "Listen to me. You are involved in this mess and will follow my orders to the letter. Are we clear?"

"Yes, Mr. Smith," Chief Messings promised.

"I'll be in touch."

Chief Messings put down the phone with a shaky hand and looked at the half-eaten donut. "Oh boy," he said in an alarmed voice. He picked up the donut and gobbled it down. "Oh boy, oh boy, oh boy, is this town in trouble."

CHAPTER FOUR

S arah stood in the relaxing spray of the hot shower until her body felt like it might melt, and then got dressed at a leisurely pace in the roomy hotel suite. She donned a warm gray sweater that complemented her knee-length black skirt. She completed the look by carefully brushing her shining hair back into a tight, no-nonsense ponytail that made her feel like a cop again. "Once a cop, always a cop," she said aloud, staring at herself with satisfaction in the large hotel room mirror.

She gazed around the luxurious suite that she and Amanda had gone halfsies on. The suite was spotless and roomy, decorated in tasteful colors and furniture. It held two plush queen size beds, a cozy sitting area, a small kitchen outfitted with chic stainless steel appliances, and a living room area with a generous window. "Almost like a small apartment," Sarah called out to Amanda as she began unpacking her things into the dresser.

"This suite would make a very nice flat in London," Amanda agreed, hanging up the blue dress that had lost out to the tan blouse and peach dress she was now wearing. "I'm starving," she added.

"Me, too." Sarah continued to neaten the contents of her suitcase, then took out her extra ammunition and moved it to the safe in the bedroom closet. Owing to the threat from the menacing mayor, she had already secured her sidearm in a thigh holster and packed her usual ankle holster away. "I'm sure by now Mr. Smith has sent someone to watch us. It would be wise if we ate lunch in the hotel restaurant."

Amanda turned and looked at Sarah. "That Mr. Smith bloke...he sure was creepy, wasn't he?"

"He's no ordinary mayor, that's for sure," Sarah concurred. She took a few seconds to study her appearance in the bureau mirror. Even though she was past forty, her beauty still shone and her eyes held plenty of beauty and fire. Lifting her hand, she touched a single strand of gray hair she spotted resting in her pretty bangs. "A gray hair," she sighed and walked away from the mirror. "I'm going to call Conrad's room."

"I wouldn't," Amanda warned.

Sarah turned to watch Amanda walk into the small

kitchen and open the refrigerator tucked into the corner. "Why not?"

"Hey, this hotel put some goodies in here," Amanda exclaimed happily.

Sarah leaned against the doorway between the bedroom and the kitchen area and watched her best friend explore the complimentary gifts in the refrigerator as the sound of heavily falling rain filled the suite. "Why shouldn't I call Conrad's room?" she asked again.

Amanda looked up, now with a bright red apple in her hand. "Because," she said, tossing the apple impishly to Sarah, "Conrad doesn't need a mother, love. He'll be along shortly."

"Mother?" Sarah repeated defensively. "I don't treat Conrad like I'm his mother."

"Of course not, silly." Amanda smiled indulgently at her friend before she stuck her head back into the refrigerator. "All I'm saying is that this case is tugging on Conrad's heart more than ours, and he doesn't need us breathing down his neck."

Sarah understood. She took a bite of the apple in her hand and thought about Mickey Slate and his long-ago past with Conrad. She thought about how the two men had once been close friends, standing side by side on the tough streets of New York. Conrad had a history with Mickey that went deeper than she could understand.

"I've been thinking...Mickey Slate was definitely murdered," she told Amanda, "but..."

"But?" Amanda asked, closing the refrigerator door with her right foot while holding a bottle of ginger ale in one hand and an apple in the other.

"Proving that he was murdered is going to be very tough," Sarah confessed. "The body—and I don't mean to sound impersonal—Mr. Slate has been cremated."

"That's really bad, huh?"

"Yes," Sarah said in a serious voice. "At best, we can attempt to search out whatever witnesses may be daring enough to speak to us and put together a few pieces, but without a body...forensic data...verified toxicology reports...we're not going to get very far."

Amanda set the bottle of ginger ale on the glossy marble counter. "Conrad knows this, too?"

"Of course." Sarah watched as Amanda stuck the apple she was holding into her teeth, opened the bottle of ginger ale, and then removed the apple from her mouth again. Even though Amanda was her own age, Sarah mused fondly, there was a childlike innocence to the woman that somehow seemed to let her travel ten years back in time. "I'm not quite certain what Conrad's plan is. Right now, the odds are not in our favor. We're liable to create some very lethal enemies for ourselves along the way, too."

Amanda nodded as she took a drink of her ginger ale. "Call me crazy, but I think we need to start back at the Snowflake Inn," she told Sarah in a thoughtful voice. "We need to put that miserable bloke who owns the joint under some serious heat."

Amanda's serious expression and tough voice made Sarah grin. "Okay, Columbo," she teased, "I'll bring the heat and you bring the gas."

Amanda rolled her eyes. "You cops." She walked over to the sitting area. Plopping down on the comfortable white couch, she waited for Sarah to join her—but before Sarah could sit down, someone knocked on the door to the suite. "There's Conrad," she said with an I-told-you-so tone of voice.

Sarah eased over to the door, looked through the security peephole, and saw Conrad standing in the hallway. She unlocked the door to let him in. "Is everything okay?" she asked.

Conrad gestured toward the third-floor elevators. "Snyder's two goons are down in the lobby. I've been watching them for a bit," he explained. Looking worried, he did not step forward to enter the suite. "Those guys are deadly, Sarah, but right now they won't make a move unless ordered."

Sarah quickly scanned Conrad's haggard appearance. It was clear that he hadn't showered or even rested. "They can stay in the lobby, then. Meanwhile, we can grab lunch in the hotel restaurant."

"I was thinking the same thing," Conrad said. He shoved his hands into the pockets of his black leather jacket and looked at Sarah. "We need to speak with Dean before he ends up missing or dead. We'll order to go and eat on the way to the motel."

Amanda appeared in the doorway behind Sarah. She too saw Conrad's haggard face and then looked at his hair, still damp from the rain. "Listen, Mr. Tough Guy, you need to take a breather. We'll eat at this lovely hotel and then go out to the Snowflake Inn."

"I wouldn't argue with her," Sarah cautioned.

Conrad knew that he needed to let his mind rest for at least a few minutes. Taking a quick break in a restaurant filled with music, comfortable tables, and delicious food didn't sound half bad, either. "Okay," he agreed begrudgingly, "maybe we can take a thirty minute lunch break."

"Great," Amanda beamed. "Meet us in the restaurant in ten minutes."

"Okay," Conrad said, momentarily confused, as the two women in front of him appeared dressed and ready to go. He gave a quizzical look to Sarah, who shrugged her shoulders, and then he walked back to the elevators, chalking it up to the mysteries of women. Sarah closed the door and immediately turned to her friend. "Why didn't we just walk down with Conrad?" she asked Amanda suspiciously. "I'm ready now."

"Oh, no you're not, love," said Amanda with a grin. She ran into the bedroom, grabbed a pink bottle of perfume from the wooden nightstand, and dashed back to Sarah. Before Sarah could say a word, Amanda spritzed her with the perfume. "There," Amanda said happily, "now we're ready to eat."

Sarah lifted her sweater to sniff the perfume. It smelled of roses, baby powder and a hint of cinnamon. "What kind of perfume did you spray on me?" she begged.

"Moonlight Flowers," Amanda said. She winked at Sarah. "No reason why I can't play matchmaker while we're on our case."

"We're investigating a homicide, June Bug, not taking a cruise on the Love Boat."

"Who says love can't blossom in Minnesota?" Amanda said with a triumphant smile as she left the room to return the perfume to the nightstand.

"Oh boy," Sarah sighed and then sniffed her sweater again. "As Charlie Brown would say: good grief."

"Come on," Amanda said in an excited voice, "Conrad is waiting."

"June Bug...Amanda...please," Sarah begged. "Conrad's

mind is not on romance and neither is mine. I'm far from ready to think about becoming involved in a relationship again."

"I know, I know," Amanda said gently. "I understand." She took Sarah's hand and looked deep into her friend's eyes. "I'm not proposing you and Conrad become engaged today, love."

"Then what are you proposing?"

"All I'm proposing is that two very lonely people have a nice lunch together," Amanda said in a loving voice. "Okay?"

Sarah looked into Amanda's warm, caring eyes. "Okay, June Bug," she said. "Now, let's go get something to eat."

They took the elevator down to the first floor, then walked through the wide and spacious lobby filled with tall, bright green plants rising above the white marble floor. "Interstate hotels are always nice," she commented to Amanda. As she was admiring the decor, Sarah spotted Snyder's two men talking to each other near the front desk. The entrance to the restaurant was on the far side of the lobby, giving Sarah enough time as they crossed the lobby to make it known to Snyder's men that she was aware of them as she walked by. The two men glared malevolently at Sarah.

"There's Conrad," Amanda said, sounding grateful.

Sarah saw Conrad standing at the entrance of the restaurant, waiting with his arms folded. He cast a quick eye at Snyder's men and then focused on Sarah and Amanda. "I already got us a table in the back," he said. "Not a whole lot on the menu, but it'll do. I thought I would come out and wait for you two since the other welcoming committee out here didn't look too friendly."

Sarah suppressed a smile at this joke, but she was grateful to Conrad. She followed Conrad as he led them to the back of the small restaurant with a pinkish-white marble floor and simple furnishings and decor. It held clusters of square tables nestled up against each other like bickering siblings. The space was cramped, but Sarah didn't mind. She liked the atmosphere, and she especially liked the white piano shoved into the corner, where an elderly man was caressing the piano keys with talented fingers, playing a jazz song.

"We have the place all to ourselves," Amanda said in a delighted voice. When Conrad walked them to the table, Amanda quickly urged Sarah toward the table first. "You sit down here," she said, "and I'll sit here. Conrad, you sit right there."

Conrad gave Sarah an "oh no" look but sat down in the spot Amanda had requested. Sarah rolled her eyes good-naturedly and sat down next to him. "She sprayed me down with her perfume," she whispered to him as Amanda sat down across from them.

Conrad sniffed Sarah and then grinned. "You smell like a flower garden full of babies."

"I know," Sarah said and then suddenly found herself blushing. Perhaps it had something to do with the fact that Conrad had never gotten quite that close to her before.

"So," Amanda began as she scanned the menu, but stopped abruptly when she spotted Snyder's two men walk into the restaurant, look around, and take a table near the entrance. "My, that didn't take long."

A woman walked out of the swinging door leading into the kitchen. Spotting Sarah and her group and then looking over at Snyder's two men, the woman seemed to make a decision. She approached the detectives' table. "My name is Norma," she told them in a bored voice. "I'll be your waitress. What can I start you off with to drink?"

Sarah looked up at Norma. The woman had to be at least sixty, she thought. "Coffee, please."

Amanda frowned. She didn't care for the wrinkled brown uniform Norma was wearing. And, as she examined Norma's grumpy features, she itched to take a comb and curlers to the woman's short, messy gray hair—but it would take more than a little Midnight Flowers to do something about the smell of cigarette smoke lingering on the woman's clothes. She sighed. "Coffee for me, too."

"Coffee," Conrad said, "black."

"I would like some cream and sugar," Amanda said quickly.

"Me, too," Sarah said.

Norma ran her tongue along her gums, her upper lip bulging. "Today's special is meatloaf and mashed potatoes," she said, nodding her head at the menus sitting on the table. "Everything else is on the menu if you are not interested in the special."

Norma's voice was robotic with boredom. It was clear to Sarah that she had said the same words so many times she probably didn't even have to think about it.

"I'll go with a cheeseburger and some fries."

"Same here," Amanda added.

"Cheeseburgers and fries all around, well done, skip the mayo and onion," Conrad requested.

Norma raised her eyebrows, nodded, and wandered over to Snyder's men. Sarah watched as one of them told Norma to take a hike. The man's hostile tone and cruel expression brought fear to Norma's face. She quickly hurried back to the kitchen. "We're not going to get very far with those two tagging us all day," Sarah told Conrad in a low voice.

"Yep," Conrad said. He slid his eyes over to the two men, who returned his look with faces that could make a grizzly bear slink away in fear, and wondered how he was going to slip free of their grip.

Amanda glanced over her shoulder to look at one of the men, stuck out her tongue, and then looked back at Conrad. "Anything?" she asked in a hushed voice.

Conrad sighed. "Amanda," he whispered, "those two guys are trained killers. Let's not irritate them, okay?"

"Please don't antagonize them," Sarah begged.

"Fine." Amanda pouted and crossed her arms.

Conrad spotted a tall, fat man in a navy blue police uniform walk into the restaurant, pause to study Snyder's men, then scoot awkwardly around them as if they were poisonous. He made his way over to the detectives' table. "Detectives Spencer, Garland, and Funnel?" Chief Messings asked in a polite voice.

Amanda looked up at the police chief and wondered what beanstalk this gigantic man had fallen from. Seeing the smirk on Amanda's face, Sarah shot her friend a desperate look and shook her head. Amanda rolled her eyes. "Yes?" she answered simply, instead of asking why he was apparently an enemy of healthy food.

Chief Messings offered a cheesy smile. "My name is Chief Messings, Winneshabba Chief of Police. Can I sit down?"

"If the chair will hold you," Amanda coughed into her

hand. Sarah kicked her ankle under the table. Amanda winced in pain but also suppressed a smile.

The chief pulled out the fourth chair at the table and sat down next to Amanda, his cheeks a little pink as he avoided looking at her. Sarah realized with chagrin that he had overheard Amanda's unsubtle joke. "Is something the matter, Chief Messings?" Sarah asked politely.

Chief Messings shifted in his chair, glancing with lightning-fast eyes at Snyder's thugs and then back at Sarah. "I was told you three are here because of Mickey Slate?" he asked, his tone aiming for professional and serious, but Sarah could see he wasn't very good at hiding his nerves.

"Mickey Slate was a close friend," Conrad answered. "I believe he was murdered, and I intend to find out why and by whom."

Sarah felt like kicking Conrad for his bluntness but didn't. She knew he was handling the case his way, and she had promised to respect that. "We're looking for answers," she chimed in after Conrad in a more cordial voice. "We were very upset to find out that the body had been cremated."

Chief Messings fidgeted in his seat, then swiveled to watch as Norma emerged from the back of the restaurant carrying three white cups of coffee on a brown tray.

"Chief Messings, what brings you here?" she asked, setting the coffee mugs onto the table.

"Business," he replied. "Bring me a cup of java, will you?"

"And some cream and sugar," Amanda reminded Norma. Norma gave Amanda a sour look and hurried back into the kitchen.

"Are you here on official business?" Chief Messings asked Conrad.

"Maybe," Conrad answered, taking a slow sip of his coffee. "My people back in New York are interested in knowing who killed Mickey. We also have people in London and Anchorage."

Chief Messings frowned. "New York, London, and Anchorage?" he repeated.

Sarah didn't blame him for his skepticism. He might be a bit of a buffoon, but Conrad's straight talk made it clear that tourism was a flimsy cover story at best.

Conrad nodded his head. "Detective Garland has her people in Los Angeles. Detective Funnel has her people in London. My people are in New York. We're here working—that is, visiting—as a team."

Chief Messings' frown deepened. "I see." He bit down on his lower lip. "Well...I hope you find the answers you need."

Amanda grinned at Conrad and decided to test the chief. "Actually, you can help us with something. We want to talk with a suspect," she explained.

"A suspect?" Chief Messings asked as the polite smile faded from his face.

"Yes," Sarah said, hoping Amanda's gambit would prove to be successful. She chose her words with care. "You know how it is in a hotel..." she tilted her head in the direction of Snyder's men without looking at them. "You never know who's listening. We would like to use your facilities for questioning, if possible."

At that moment, one of Snyder's men abruptly stood up and walked out of the restaurant with his phone at his ear. The second man remained seated, his attention focused squarely on Chief Messings. Sarah watched the portly police chief swallow uncomfortably.

"Well...I, uh..." he struggled to speak. "No promises, but maybe we can talk down at the station, huh, detectives?" he asked hopefully.

"Of course," Sarah said in a professional tone, and watched as he seemed to take a breath in relief.

Chief Messings looked at her. "You're kinda famous," he commented. "I remember seeing you on the news."

"Oh?" Sarah asked, even though she knew exactly what Chief Messings was referring to.

"Don't act so humble," he said. "It's not every day someone catches a serial killer. You single-handedly captured the Alley Killer. That's impressive." She realized too late that his excited voice was easily audible across the small restaurant. Perhaps it wasn't anything that Snyder's men didn't already know about her. Still, she felt the need to tamp down his enthusiasm.

"The Los Angeles Police Department captured the Alley Killer, Chief Messings. I couldn't have made a move without the help of every single police officer and the other team members that offered their valuable services. Police officers work as a team and that's what matters the most."

Conrad nodded his head, appreciating Sarah's fast wit and ability to push Chief Messings into a corner. He moved forward. "You know, *your* cooperation in this case would be very helpful, Chief Messings. We can work together as a team."

The chief's face went pale. "Uh...right now I'm...well, busy with other...duties. I will do what I can to help, of course, but my time is very valuable."

Sarah decided to test him even further. "We understand. Maybe you can help us with something else, however. That man sitting over there has been harassing us ever since we got here. Would you please tell him to leave?"

Chief Messings froze in his seat. His eyes slowly rotated

to Snyder's man as if considering him for the first time. "I..." he tried to speak. "I...well...he seems...perfectly peaceful at the moment."

Norma walked over to the table and followed Chief Messings' glance. "That creep told me to get lost," she said with no subtlety, her complaint carrying clearly across the empty restaurant. "All I did was ask him what he would like to drink. If he's not a paying customer, he's the one who needs to get lost."

Chief Messings swallowed. "I..." Sarah watched as beads of sweat gathered on his forehead. "I..." His hand drifted down to his belt and he made a twitching movement as if to adjust it.

In that moment, Snyder's thug stood up and walked out of the restaurant. If Sarah hadn't been watching closely, she almost would have missed the signal that had passed between the two men.

"And stay out," Norma said to the man's retreating back. She handed Chief Messings his coffee. "Your cheeseburgers will be out in a few minutes."

"Make them to go," Conrad said and picked up his coffee cup. "Chief Messings," he said in a firm voice, "I need a background report on a man named Snyder Smith."

Chief Messings' eyes nearly bulged from his head. "Mayor Smith is a well-respected citizen in this town," he said weakly. "I...can't do anything without a court order."

Sarah picked up her coffee and took a sip. Amanda did the same, giving up hope on ever receiving her cream and sugar. So what if the coffee was black, she thought. If Los Angeles could handle it, then so could she. "So get a court order," she said.

"On what grounds?" Chief Messings asked nervously.

Conrad decided to take advantage of the situation and bait a second line. "We believe Snyder Smith may be connected to McCallister Security."

The chief turned to give Conrad a bewildered look. "Who?" he asked.

"McCallister Security," Conrad repeated. "Mickey Slate worked for McCallister Security, in their legal department."

Sarah scanned the police chief's pallid face. The large man seemed to have no clue what Conrad was talking about, which meant, she knew, that this was a dead end for now. "Chief Messings, we'll work on getting the court order you need to run a check on Snyder Smith for us. What judge do we need to speak with?"

Chief Messings took a gulp of coffee and stood up. "I'm afraid I have to go. I'm a very busy man. We can talk more down at the station. Good day," he said and hurried away.

"Weasel," Amanda whispered.

"Yep," Conrad agreed.

"Totally," Sarah added and grew silent as her mind began to sift through possibilities.

A few minutes later, Norma brought the cheeseburgers and fries out in three white plastic to-go boxes. So much for their relaxing lunch break. Sarah went back up to the suite, gathered her and Amanda's coats along with an umbrella, and hurried back down into the lobby. "Snyder's men aren't around right now," she noted to Conrad in an undertone, handing Amanda her coat.

"Yep," Conrad said. He held out the three to-go boxes. "We'd better move."

Amanda took the umbrella from Sarah and followed her outside into the rainy parking lot. "The rain is coming down even harder," she observed, raising the umbrella over her head.

Sarah hunched under the umbrella and cast her eyes at the low, dark gray sky. "It's cold enough to snow," she said, following Conrad to the rental SUV.

"We don't need snow right now," Conrad said as he walked past a shiny red Dodge Charger with California license plates. Sarah spotted the license plates and slowed down. A sad expression flitted across her face.

"Are you okay?"

"Huh?" Sarah asked, still staring at the license plate.

71

Images of her ex-husband driving his black BMW down their neighborhood street pushed themselves into her mind.

"Come on, love." Amanda pushed Sarah past the car.

Sarah sighed and climbed into the SUV. "We'd better hurry to the motel," she told Conrad as she quickly buckled up, but Conrad was already focused, starting the car and backing out of the parking lot. She caught a glimpse of his steely eyes in the rearview mirror.

Amanda, nestled in the back seat with the three to-go boxes, waited until Conrad had driven out of the half-full parking lot before handing out the food. "Here, love," she told Sarah.

Reluctantly, Sarah took her to-go box and opened it. "I'm not really hungry anymore."

"Eat," Conrad echoed, taking his box from Amanda with one careful hand. "If Dean over at the Snowflake Inn got in trouble with Snyder, we could be driving to a homicide scene, Sarah. We need our energy."

"Please eat, love," Amanda pleaded. She said a prayer of thanks for the food. "Amen."

"Amen," Sarah and Conrad whispered.

Conrad took his cheeseburger out of the to-go box and took a big bite, keeping the steering wheel steady with his other hand. "Chief Messings is bought and paid for," he commented. "But there's room to manipulate his puppet strings."

"I think so, too," Sarah agreed.

None of them said another word until Conrad pulled the SUV into the filthy parking lot connected to the Snowflake Inn. "Careful now," Sarah said, darting her eyes around to check the corners, "Snyder's men could be anywhere."

Amanda polished off the last of her fries, closed the to-go box in her lap, set it aside, and looked out of the rain-spotted front windshield. The only other vehicle she could see in the parking lot was a sedan that had seen better days. It probably belonged to the owner of the motel. She waited until Conrad had parked next to the vehicle before she spoke. "Maybe I should wear a gun?"

Conrad looked at Sarah, who nodded her head. "Okay." Conrad bent forward and retrieved his backup weapon, a small 9 mm Luger, from his right ankle holster. "The gun is loaded and ready to fire."

Amanda stared at the gun and then, feeling slightly uneasy, took it from Conrad. "Show me how to fire this baby," she said.

Conrad quickly showed Amanda the safety mechanism and how to fire the gun if and when needed. "Got it?"

"Got it," Amanda said, sliding the gun into the empty to-go box sitting next to her. "You guys ready?"

Sarah stared out into the rain falling hard on the pavement. Her gut told her exactly what was waiting for them in the motel lobby: a dead body. "Let's move," she said and opened the car door.

Conrad jumped out of the SUV. He scanned the parking lot and the empty motel rooms, then focused his eyes directly on the worn, shabby building that served as the Snowflake Inn's lobby. "Let's go," he said, ignoring the rain.

"Leave the umbrella," Sarah called out to Amanda as she jogged after Conrad.

Amanda wasn't in the mood to get soaking wet, but she did as Sarah asked. Racing out of the back seat with the to-go box in her hand, she chased after Sarah as the cold rain saturated her hair and ran down her face. Conrad glanced over his shoulder and saw Amanda running to catch up. When he reached the green door, he stopped and waited for his companions. "Look," he said, nodding at the door.

Sarah examined the door in the harsh glare of the light from the lone streetlight. The paint of the door was peeling off, but that wasn't what caught her eye: the wood around the lock was slightly splintered. Without a word, she withdrew her gun from her holster and nodded her head at Conrad. "Let's get in there."

Conrad looked at Amanda. "Take your gun out of that silly box and be ready for action," he told her.

With nervous hands, Amanda retrieved her gun and threw down the to-go box. Suddenly she no longer felt excited; instead, she felt terrified. "Okay...let's...get in there," she said, taking a deep breath and trying to ignore the knot in her stomach.

Conrad nodded. Using his right shoulder, he rammed the door open and charged into the front lobby, which reeked of cigarette smoke and stale beer. With his gun at the ready, he searched the room. "Clear," he called out over his shoulder.

Sarah ran across the dirty brown carpet toward the green linoleum front desk counter. Behind the front counter sat a shabby recliner with its back to the lobby so it could face an aging television that was still blaring. On the small desk behind the counter was a mess of papers, hotel room keys, and dirty ashtrays. Drawing in a deep breath, she stood on tiptoe to look down at the recliner. "Body," she called out in a neutral voice that somehow still betrayed the strain of her discovery.

Conrad ran to the front counter and looked over. The body of Hank Dean was sitting in the recliner as an old episode of *Family Feud* blared on. Only now, Hank Dean wasn't calling out quick and senseless answers to the questions like he used to do. Now, the man was sitting very silent and very still. "Stupid lunch break," Conrad swore under his breath. A pattern of dark, sickly bruises were clearly visible around the man's neck, and his head lolled to one side at an unnatural angle.

"We can't take the blame for this," Sarah told Conrad sternly. Sarah took a calming breath and looked closer. "Look at the size of those marks. Must have come from some pretty big fingers." She frowned. Turning away from the front counter, she examined the lobby. The walls were lined with wood paneling that was peeling in places. The lobby was devoid of furniture, artwork, or anything else to relieve the atmosphere. Shaking her head, she turned to examine the body in the recliner again. "Okay," she said to Conrad. "Let's get to work."

Conrad shook his head. "How?" he asked. "No one in this town is going to help us, Sarah." He looked over his shoulder at Amanda. "Stay near the door and keep an eye out. I'm going to check out Dean's apartment. Sarah, you're with me."

"But..." Amanda protested.

"If you see anything or anyone, fire a warning shot and we'll come running," Conrad promised.

"No way," Sarah objected. "Amanda and I stay together at all times. Besides, she's never fired that gun before, do you really want to take that chance? We'll investigate Dean's apartment, Conrad. You stay here."

Conrad considered this and then nodded his head. "Okay, go," he said. He walked to the front door. "Be careful," he warned Amanda.

"I will," Amanda promised, relieved. She followed Sarah through a door on the far back wall of the lobby. "Wow, what stinks?" she exclaimed, grabbing her nose with her right hand.

"I don't know," Sarah said, and cautiously moved down the short, carpeted hallway. The hallway ended in a cramped room containing an unmade bed, a couch that looked as if it had come from the local landfill, a rusted stove and a crooked kitchen table. Walking over the shaggy, cigarette-burned brown carpet, she made her way toward the stove and stopped. "Stove is on," she said. "Stand back."

Amanda took a step back and watched Sarah pull the stove door open. Black smoke exploded from the oven. Amanda coughed and covered her nose. "Oh, so that's the awful smell."

Sarah fanned at the smoke and turned off the stove. When the smoke cleared, she bent down and studied the interior of the oven. A smoldering green trash bag sat inside like a diseased turkey. "Amanda?"

"Yes?" Amanda asked, slowly making her way over to the oven.

"We have some trash to dig through." Sarah straightened up. "Too bad the rain outside can't wash away all the trash in this world."

Amanda bent down and studied the green bag. "We have a dead body, a burned trash bag, and a police chief who's afraid of his own shadow. We're really making progress, Los Angeles."

Sarah bit down on her lower lip. "I know, June Bug, I know," she sighed. Her heart felt sick. She studied the room with sad eyes while the rain outside continued to pour down from the cold gray sky in furious torrents.

CHAPTER FIVE

Conrad carefully removed the trash bag from the oven. "I'm going to put this bag in the SUV, and then we should call Chief Messings," he told Sarah and Amanda.

Sarah didn't like tampering with a crime scene—and she especially didn't like concealing evidence—but the situation called for drastic measures. "I'll call him," she said, following Conrad back to the front lobby.

"Okay," Conrad replied with a nod, turning his collar up against the rain.

Amanda closed the door leading into the small apartment and watched Conrad walk outside. Standing in a room with a dead body in it didn't exactly make her feel safe, and the gun she was holding in her shaky hands surely didn't make her feel safe, either. "I wonder what that bloke knew?" she asked Sarah, tossing a glance toward the front counter.

"Maybe the contents of the trash bag will tell us?" Sarah suggested. She walked over to the front desk and, without looking at the recliner, leaned over the counter, picked up the brown telephone and dialed 911. "Yes, this is Detective Sarah Garland. I'm at the Snowflake Inn. The owner of the inn is dead. I need an ambulance and for you to dispatch Chief Messings to my location."

Amanda stared at Sarah. Despite all that they had been through, she had never heard her best friend speak in an official "I'm-a-cop" voice. "Impressive," she said.

Sarah put the phone back on the cradle. "Every emergency call is recorded. It's an old trick. You always want to make sure you use a tone of voice that the courts can appreciate."

"You cops," Amanda grinned. "I guess you're more than donut-eating blokes living off the taxpayer's dollar after all."

"Not all of us." Sarah tried to smile but failed. Instead, she shook her head. "I never got used to it, June Bug. In all of my years dealing with homicides, I never got used to it. Human life is so fragile and so precious...yet it's treated with contempt by so many. The heart of mankind is vicious and ugly, always lunging from dark shadows and attacking with merciless fangs."

"Is that the writer speaking or the cop?" Amanda asked gently.

Sarah sighed. "Both," she said. Keeping her back to the front counter, she carefully surveyed the front lobby. "This lobby is hideous, but to the man sitting in that recliner, this was his safe zone, his place to hide away from the world...even his home. Humans are just like other creatures, June Bug. They hide in all the cracks and spaces they can find. Alaska is our space to hide in...this motel was his."

Amanda moved to the front door to wait for Conrad, her mind still tangled with the words Sarah had spoken. "Kick over a rock...and you may find a ladybug or a spider," she said.

Sarah nodded her head. "Cities like Los Angeles are one big rock, and under that rock are ladybugs and spiders living together."

"Well," Amanda said, taking in a deep breath, "this ladybug is a fighter and I'm not afraid of spiders...moths, yes...spiders, no."

"That's my girl," Sarah said proudly.

Just then, Conrad opened the front door and walked into the lobby with Snyder Smith right behind him, holding a gun to his back.

"Drop your guns," Snyder ordered Sarah and Amanda.

"Do it," Sarah told Amanda calmly. Amanda leaned down and gingerly tossed the Luger onto the floor. Sarah waited. Maybe, she hoped, he wouldn't realize she had her own gun hidden in the holster strapped to her thigh under her knee-length skirt.

"Against the counter," Snyder said and shoved Conrad forward, too.

Sarah moved toward the counter while Snyder closed the door, cutting off the sight and sound of the heavy rain falling outside. "I already called 911. Chief Messings is on his way," she warned Snyder.

Snyder ignored her. He was dripping with rain and wearing a coldly furious expression that clearly implied he was in no mood to banter. "I didn't give the order for Hank Dean to be killed," he spoke through angrily gritted teeth. "This man was simply a washed-up hippie trapped in his own mind. You obviously saw this when you met him."

Conrad reached out and gently eased Amanda closer to Sarah and a little behind him. "Mr. Dean didn't appear completely mentally functional," he admitted.

Snyder kept his back against the door. "Obviously," he said, making a great effort to control his voice, "I have multiple problems. Someone, it appears, took it upon himself to kill Hank Dean against my wishes, which now makes me the prime suspect in your eyes."

"You killed Mickey Slate," Conrad accused, barely restraining the anger in his voice. "I don't know who killed Dean, but I do know you killed Mickey."

Sarah watched Snyder's eyes and facial expression closely. He slowly adjusted his stance and took a moment to compose himself. "Detective Spencer, I did some checking," he said, looking pointedly at Amanda. "Detective Funnel is not a detective, after all. Detective Garland is retired. And you, sir, are a lowly cop working traffic stops in a small town in Alaska. You have no right to show up in my town, where I am the mayor and a respected citizen and funeral director who conducted a normal cremation. How dare you suggest otherwise when—"

"Why did you kill Mickey?" Conrad barked. "I want answers, Snyder."

Snyder stared across the room at Conrad coldly. "Mickey Slate was not my problem," he said coldly. "The man was meant to die in New York, but he escaped and came to my so-called neck of the woods. I was ordered to kill him. I simply carried out the order."

"Ordered by whom?" Sarah asked. "McCallister?"

"Oh no," Snyder said and actually laughed to himself. "I'm not foolish enough to poke at that anthill. If Mr. McCallister had wanted Mickey Slate dead, Mickey Slate would not have escaped from New York like he did.

It wasn't McCallister, I know that much. Mickey...was a very skilled man. But not skilled enough to escape McCallister," he finished with a sneer.

Conrad felt like running across the room and punching Snyder in the face. Instead, he forced himself to remain calm. It was obvious someone in Winneshabba was working against Snyder, and he needed to find out who it was. Conrad's first suspect was Chief Messings; but would the bumbling police chief really have killed a motel owner to spite his own boss, the mayor? But first, he had a more painful and immediate question that Snyder needed to answer. "Why did Mickey have to die?"

"Why?" Snyder asked, looking as if Conrad had just slung cold water onto his face. "Detective Spencer, Mickey Slate was not the saint you perceived him to be in that twisted mind of yours."

"Skip the dramatics," Conrad snapped.

"Very well." Snyder abruptly changed his tone from cordial to cold and calculating. "Your old friend Mickey Slate was blackmailing a very powerful businessman. Why? Because Mickey had a gambling problem, that's why. He was in debt. Hundreds of thousands of dollars. He needed money and my client became his target."

"Your client?" Sarah asked.

Snyder locked eyes with Sarah. "Detective Garland, up until four years ago, I worked with a hidden group formed within the United Nations whose core responsibility was to create global policies designed to cause conflict and eventually war between nations. You can imagine that I came into contact with some very merciless people."

"You snake!" Amanda yelled.

"Perhaps," Snyder said, unfazed by Amanda's insult. He continued. "Eventually, it became time for me to...retire, as they say, due to certain internal conflicts within the United Nations. After I retired, I relocated to this small community and began my shadow business."

"You hire out mercenaries," Conrad guessed.

"Certain clients contact me when they need me to provide...extermination services, yes," Snyder explained. "However, Detective Spencer, I did not plan for Mickey to be eliminated in New York." He paused, trying to control a sudden burst of temper before spitting out, "My client took it upon herself to take a few cheap shots at him."

"*Her*self?" Sarah asked.

Snyder turned to Sarah, flustered. Realizing that his slip of the tongue had revealed a vital piece of information, he shook his head and ignored her question. "We have a mess here, do we not?" he asked. He began to pace slowly back and forth, taking his eyes off his intended victims as he did so.

Conrad glanced at Sarah. Sarah nudged Amanda and then spoke to Amanda with her eyes, nodding her head down where her gun resided in its holster.

"Oh," Amanda whispered, her eyes widening.

"Pretend to faint," Sarah whispered in a voice so faint it was almost inaudible. Amanda hesitated. She looked at Snyder, who was still muttering and pacing back and forth. Her heart raced as she realized what they were about to do. Sarah looked at Conrad, her eyes asking him if he was ready. Conrad nodded his head a fraction, keeping his eyes on Snyder. "Now," Sarah whispered to Amanda.

Amanda felt as if she really were about to faint. She let out an anguished moan and crumpled to the ground. "Amanda," Sarah cried out, dropping to her knees and slid her gun from her thigh holster in the same motion, on the side facing away from Snyder

"What now?" Snyder growled, his eyes narrowing.

"She fainted," Sarah said in a voice so believably worried that she probably deserved some kind of award. "My friend is...hypoglycemic. She hasn't eaten very much today. Her blood sugar has probably dropped below the danger line."

Snyder rolled his eyes. "Leave her be," he ordered.

Sarah rested her hand on Amanda's cheek. "She needs a

hospital," she told Snyder with false urgency, moving to feel Amanda's forehead in order to distract from what she was doing with her right.

"Stand up, now!" Snyder barked at Sarah and pointed his gun at her. "Detective Garland, I will not tell you again."

Sarah cast her eyes up and looked at Snyder. "Is asking for a doctor too much?" she begged, shifting her eyes to Conrad for a second, knowing he would take the cue.

"Yes," Snyder snapped. "Now, stand up."

Sarah slowly began to stand up, her mouth open as if to continue pleading. Now it was Conrad's turn to join in the act. "Hey!" he shouted, turning to point at the door leading to Dean's small apartment, "someone is back there!"

Snyder took his eyes off Sarah and looked at the door in sudden alarm. Sarah didn't waste a second. She dropped down to one knee and fired off a single shot. The bullet struck Snyder's right hand. He cried out in pain and dropped his gun. Instantly, Conrad charged at Snyder like a raging bull. Before Snyder could react, he was on the floor and Conrad had secured his hands in handcuffs behind his back. "My...hand..." he cried out in pain.

"Deal with it," Conrad said with a grimace, scooping the Luger up off the floor and handing it back to Amanda. "Great performance," he congratulated her.

"Thank you, thank you," Amanda said, standing up and taking a bow.

Sarah patted Amanda on the back. "You did great, June Bug," she said and then in the moment of quiet that followed, they all heard the sound of car wheels creeping across the wet pavement outside. "Someone is here."

Conrad jogged over to the door. Carefully, he eased the door open just enough to see outside into the heavy rain. "It's Messings." He watched the police chief park his blue and white patrol car next to their rental SUV and climb out.

"Put the gun away," Sarah told Amanda quickly. Amanda tucked the gun into the right pocket of her coat. "Just in case we need another distraction, lie down and don't move."

"Again?" Amanda sighed. She lay down on the floor and closed her eyes.

"Snyder, if you want to live, not a word," Sarah warned.

"You're all dead," Snyder hissed. "All I have to do is make one phone call."

"Kill us later," Sarah said, "but for now, keep your mouth shut."

"What's your plan?" Conrad asked Sarah as he continued to watch Chief Messings, who was looking in the windows of their SUV.

"Let him in," Sarah said. She backed up to the front counter and placed her gun next to the telephone. "Keep your gun out of sight."

Conrad hesitated but then decided to follow Sarah's order. "Chief Messings, in here!" he called out loudly, pushing open the heavy door.

Chief Messings looked up at the door to the motel lobby, saw Conrad waving at him, and hurried over. "I received a call from dispatch," he explained, stepping out of the heavy rain. Even though he was wearing a blue rain poncho over his uniform and a plastic cover over his hat, he was still soaking wet. "I was told someone was—" He stopped when he saw Snyder, handcuffed and lying on his stomach. The color drained from his face.

"Arrest them, Messings!" Snyder snarled in rage. "My hand! The woman shot me. I need a doctor."

"This man confessed to killing Mickey Slate," Conrad told the chief. "He tried to kill us. We acted in self-defense."

"What about her?" Chief Messings asked and pointed at Amanda with a worried finger.

"She's playing dead," Snyder cried out in frustration. "There's nothing the matter with that woman...but there will be," he warned.

"Chief Messings," Sarah spoke calmly, "more

importantly, Hank Dean is dead. His body is right behind this counter. Someone killed him."

Chief Messings immediately looked at Snyder. "I didn't order the hit," Snyder bit out.

Chief Messings hesitated, like a child stuck in a playground fight, wondering which side to take. "Mr. Snyder...sir...I..."

"Arrest these three criminals and call me an ambulance immediately," Snyder yelled. "If you refuse, you will certainly pay the penalty."

"Oh, my," Chief Messings said again in an anxious voice. "I..." He paused, removed his rain-soaked hat, and ran a meaty hand through his damp hair. "Listen," he said to Conrad, "I never wanted anything to do with this guy. One day he floats into town and begins threatening me and my wife."

"You're dead," Snyder promised.

"Maybe," Chief Messings said and shook his head, "but I'm not a killer." He turned to Sarah. "Detective Garland, I know I'm likely going to end up in jail because I covered for Mr. Smith when he sent his two men out here to kill Mickey Slate, but you have to believe me, I didn't want it to be that way. I...my wife and I...we can't have children and, well, all we have is each other. I can't let anything happen to my wife." Chief Messings looked down at Snyder. "And I knew Mr. Smith meant what he said when he promised to kill my wife first if I didn't fall in line with his sick agenda."

Sarah felt pity enter her heart. She could plainly see that the man was speaking the truth. "I understand," she said. She reached over the counter and retrieved her gun. "Amanda, stand up."

Amanda opened her eyes, looked up at Chief Messings, and stood up. "Sorry I made that joke back at the hotel," she said.

"It's okay. That chair deserved it," Chief Messings said with a wry grin. He focused his attention back on Sarah. "I don't think you fully understand," he told her. "Detective Garland, Winneshabba is such a small town here in Minnesota that if you weren't looking, you'd just drive right past the town and not even know it was here. If it weren't for the chain hotels and restaurants out there on the interstate, no one would even know Winneshabba existed."

"What are you trying to say?" Sarah asked.

Chief Messings ran his hand through his hair again. "Who could I, the police chief of this tiny, insignificant town, have gone to for help, if my own boss and mayor is corrupt? The state police, where Snyder has more of his people who can make investigations just...disappear? The state attorney general, who gets campaign contributions from Snyder every year? I didn't want to help Mr.

Smith...the thug...but what choice did I have? And I had my wife to think about."

Conrad walked over to Chief Messings and put a hand on the man's shoulder. "I think any jury will see it the same way," he promised. "You did the best you could between a rock and a hard place. And I'm going to do everything in my power to help you."

Chief Messings turned and shook Conrad's hand with enthusiasm. "Thank you," he said sincerely. "I was thinking, if I'm cleared, then I'll take my wife and move away to someplace that's safe for us."

Sarah walked over to Chief Messings and looked him in his eyes. "We still need your help, Chief Messings. Please. Someone killed Hank Dean and we have to find out who."

"My men will have you six feet under by nightfall," Snyder warned Sarah, twisting in his uncomfortable prone position on the filthy carpet to try to fix them with a glare. "Messings, you're a dead man. All of you are dead."

"Oh, change the record," Amanda griped. "You know you've been caught. You sound like a child moaning over spilt milk. Why don't you crawl back into the alley you came out of, you slimy rat?"

Chief Messings regarded Snyder with a look of dread.

"But he means it. He'll order his men to kill us, even from behind bars, and they will."

"Right now, let's focus on who killed Hank Dean," Conrad said. "In the meantime, let's lock Snyder in a closet. If he can't be found, he can't order his men to kill, now can he?"

Chief Messings actually smiled. "No, I guess they can't."

"Come on and help me," Conrad said. Sarah found a bottle of rubbing alcohol and a clean rag in the corner of the front counter and used it to rinse Snyder's bloody hand, still handcuffed. She wrapped the rag expertly around his hand to staunch the blood and secured it in a firm knot.

Sarah watched Conrad and Chief Messings pick Snyder up and stand him on his feet. "Take him to one of the motel rooms and lock him in a bathroom," she said. "His hand will need some more attention later, but he'll live for now."

"And then what?" Chief Messings asked, holding Snyder in place with a tough hand.

"Then," Sarah said, "pretend Snyder didn't happen here. Call your people and deal with the murder. Act like you don't know anything." Sarah turned to Snyder. "The person who killed Hank Dean called you, didn't they? And that person told you we were here at the motel, too."

"You're a very bright woman," Snyder said sarcastically, "but your brains won't keep you alive, Detective Garland." His eyes shifted from side to side as if expecting someone to burst into the room any moment.

"Maybe...maybe not," Sarah replied, watching Snyder, "but I think it's safe to say that the person who killed Hank Dean is close by." She looked at Conrad. "Go ahead and lock him away."

"You're dead," Snyder said in a final threat. Sarah could hear the note of desperation in Snyder's voice, but she detected something else, as well—an undercurrent of fear. Could it be that whoever killed Hank Dean was also a threat to Snyder?

"Let's go," Conrad said. He and Chief Messings pulled Snyder outside into the harsh, pouring rain.

CHAPTER SIX

*T*wo hours later, Sarah and Amanda walked into a cozy coffee shop situated near the tea house on Main Street. Sitting down at a wood table nestled in a corner, Sarah took in a deep breath of the rich, dark aroma of coffee. "Smells wonderful in here," she sighed as she removed her coat.

"Lovely," Amanda agreed, taking in the sight of the mouth-watering pastries sitting in a glass case under the front counter. This coffee shop was far different from Sarah's shop back home, she thought. Sarah's coffee shop was more for lumberjacks and hunters, while this one was designed for a very different crowd, apparently. The light brown wallpaper was in an attractive little coffee cup pattern and the floors were a glossy hardwood that reflected an equally glossy expanse of tables and bookshelves. The bookshelves held an impressive array of modern novels and musical instruments. In the back corner were a couple tables with fancy computers where people could check their email while enjoying their coffee. "Not like your coffee shop back home, eh, love?"

Sarah frowned. "No," she admitted, exploring the place with her eyes. "Maybe I can learn a few lessons from this place. It sure wouldn't hurt for me to improve the decor of my shop."

"I wholeheartedly agree," Amanda said. "No offense," she added quickly.

"None taken."

Amanda spotted a pretty young waitress with short brown hair approaching them. "I hope Conrad is okay."

"Me, too," Sarah said. She put on a fake smile when the waitress neared the table.

"Hello, my name is Ali," the waitress smiled. "What can I get you? Today's special is the Rainy Day Surprise."

"Oh?" Sarah asked.

Ali smiled apologetically and leaned forward. "Coffee flavored with a mixture of cinnamon and iced tea...one of my mother's creations," she lowered her voice. "I have to tell customers about it, but...I would recommend another drink."

Sarah smiled at Ali. The girl was sweet. "I'll have a black coffee with a blueberry muffin."

"I'll have the same, love," Amanda said, "but add a little cream and sugar to mine, please."

"Two coffees and two muffins," Ali said cheerfully and walked away.

"That old bat back at the hotel could learn a thing or two from that girl," Amanda told Sarah.

"I agree," Sarah grinned. She looked toward the front window. Night was falling, and the rain was slowly turning into snow. "I hope my plan works."

"We did find that phone number in the garbage bag," Amanda pointed out.

"But that's all we found," Sarah countered. "Hank Dean must have been in a panic when he shoved the bag into the stove. The man wasn't exactly mentally sharp."

"But," Amanda said, "if Dean was trying to get rid of something in the trash bag, he must have known that his life was in danger."

Sarah nodded her head. "It seems that way," she said and rested her chin down onto the palm of her right hand. "The phone number belonged to a payphone. You were listening on the other line when I called, right?" Amanda nodded. "When I called the number, a woman answered and then hung up. That's all we have to go on."

"You're thinking the woman who answered is the same woman who hired that rat Snyder, aren't you?" Amanda asked.

"I'm not really sure," Sarah confessed. "But if the person who killed Hank Dean was watching the motel, he or she might have tailed us here. It's unlikely anyone from town is making their way out for coffee at this time of day, in this weather."

"You mean we may have more eyes watching us than we think."

Sarah nodded. "And it all points directly to Mickey Slate." She bit her lip and looked at Amanda. "Can I confess something to you?"

"Always," Amanda said and leaned forward curiously. "Okay, Los Angeles, spill the beans. What's on your mind?"

"Hank Dean was strangled to death," she whispered. "And he wasn't killed by a woman, I know that much. I also know that Snyder was alerted to the fact that we were at the motel. But," she added, "I think he was sent to the motel to become a victim himself."

"You mean whoever killed Dean was hoping we'd get into a shootout with Snyder and kill him into the bargain?"

"I'm not sure, but it's a possibility. That's why I asked Conrad to stay back at the motel and watch the room where Snyder is locked in. June Bug, we're dealing with multiple people here and we have to play smart."

Amanda cleared her throat and nodded her head. "Here comes our order."

"Here you go," Ali smiled as she placed two green coffee mugs down onto the table, then handed Sarah and Amanda two white plates holding delicious blueberry muffins. "We close in about an hour, so there's no rush."

"Thanks," Sarah said and reached down into her purse. She pulled out a twenty dollar bill and held it up for Ali. "Here's your tip."

"Thank you," Ali said in a shocked but happy voice.

"Now, may I ask you a favor?"

"Sure," Ali said, taking the twenty-dollar bill.

"If anyone else comes in for coffee, can you use your cell phone and take a photo of that person for me?" Sarah asked. She briefly introduced herself and explained that she was a detective from out of town. "I don't want you to be alarmed, okay? All I want you to do is take a few photos for me."

Ali stared at Sarah and then, to Sarah's relief, the girl smiled excitedly. "Oh, finally some excitement in this drab little town! I'll be happy to take the photos, Detective Garland."

"You're sweet." Amanda beamed at Ali, reached into her purse and pulled out a second twenty-dollar bill. "Here you go, love, you earned it."

"Wow, thanks," Ali said warmly. "Okay, I'll go hide in the kitchen and peep my head out every few minutes."

Just as Ali hurried away, a woman with long red hair wearing a black leather trench coat entered the coffee shop. "Wow," Amanda breathed, "get a look at her."

Sarah watched as the woman sat down at a table close to the front door without removing her jacket. The only item the woman removed was her black leather biker's cap, which was dusted with a bit of snow. "Don't stare," Sarah whispered. She said a quick prayer of thanks over her muffin. "Eat."

Amanda picked up her muffin and took a bite. The woman, she saw out of the corner of her eye, looked around the coffee shop and then glanced at their table. "Hey," Amanda said and offered a friendly wave. "I see it's starting to snow."

The woman ignored Amanda, looked around again, and then stood up. Sarah watched as the woman walked to the front door, engaged the lock, and pulled a gun out of her front jacket pocket. "Hands in the air," she ordered in an icy voice.

Sarah felt her blood run cold and tried to control herself,

for Amanda's sake. Her friend's eyes were wide with shock and she had dropped her muffin mid-bite. They both turned when they heard the kitchen door open. A man with dark black hair then pushed Ali into the main room. "Mickey Slate?" Sarah cried in disbelief, her control gone.

Mickey Slate walked Ali around the front counter and shoved her toward the table. The man, Sarah saw, was hardened and tough, just as in the photograph Conrad had showed her, yet his eyes seemed to hold a touch of fear and regret. "I didn't want it to be this way," he said in a thick Brooklyn accent.

Sarah watched as Mickey pulled a gun out of the right pocket of his leather jacket. He trained it on Ali and gestured for her to sit with Sarah and Amanda. Under the table, Sarah reached for Ali's hand and gave her a reassuring squeeze. The poor girl silently shook in fright, but seemed to take comfort.

Sarah's mind was racing. "But—the cremation—"

"Snyder knew he killed the wrong man. That's why he had the body cremated."

"Why would you let Conrad think you were dead? He was grieving."

Mickey glanced over at the red-haired woman guarding the door and then back at Sarah. "You have to make tough choices," he said. "Melinda and I did what we had to in order to protect our daughter."

Sarah looked at the red-haired woman in dawning comprehension. So this was Mickey's wife—and she was in on the whole plan. "You mean to protect your daughter from being kidnapped until you've paid your gambling debts," Sarah countered. "Nobody forced you to gamble all your money away. That was your decision alone."

Melinda Slate pointed her gun at Sarah wildly. "My husband made a few mistakes. How's that any of your business?" she charged.

Sarah held her hands up in the air. "I'm just trying to figure things out," she said calmly.

"So if you're alive," Amanda asked Mickey in confusion, ignoring the gun pointed at her, "then what poor bloke was cremated?"

"A homeless man," Mickey said in a voice filled with regret. Mickey stared at Sarah. "Snyder had to think I was dead. And so did McCallister's daughter, who ordered the hit."

Sarah nodded her head. "So you were involved with McCallister Security after all."

Mickey reached up and scratched his rugged face. "Carly McCallister was selling information to a foreign company. I was the only person who knew." Mickey looked at his wife in shame. "So I blackmailed her. I...had gambling debts that needed to be paid."

Melinda reached out and took Mickey's free hand. "It's okay, baby."

Mickey nodded and looked back at Sarah. "But I pressed McCallister's daughter too hard and demanded too much money." Mickey took a breath to steady himself. "She sent someone to kill me, but I escaped. Then she sent someone to kill me and my family, but I was waiting. That's when she contacted Snyder."

"To finish the job," Sarah said.

Mickey nodded again. "I knew I wouldn't stand a chance against Snyder. And as I said, the people I owed money to were already planning to kidnap my daughter unless I paid up. I was in a real mess."

"Why did you call Conrad from New York, after the first attempt on your life?" Sarah asked.

"Yeah," Amanda chimed in. "Did you think your old street gang would protect you?"

"So Conrad told you about the Blades, huh?" Mickey said with a tired half-smile. "Yeah, Conrad and I go way back. He was the only person I could turn to for help. I called him because I needed him to watch over my daughter while my wife and I handled Snyder. But I never got the chance to ask Conrad about that."

"Where is your daughter now?" Sarah asked.

"Safe," Melinda said defensively. "Mickey, we have to do something. We can't leave them alive. They know too much and we have Macey to think about."

"I know," Mickey said, his eyes suddenly darkening. "You know I killed Hank Dean?" he asked Sarah.

"Yes."

Amanda looked at Melinda suddenly. "Hey, you're the chick who answered the payphone."

"I didn't know it was you calling," Melinda explained, keeping her voice cold. "I thought..."

Sarah waited, but Melinda didn't continue. "You thought what?" she prompted, curious.

"None of your business," Melinda snapped. "Mickey, shoot them and let's get out of here. We'll go back to the motel and finish off Snyder."

"Conrad is watching Snyder," Mickey said, his brow furrowing with anger and frustration. "It wasn't supposed to be this way. I can't go against my old friend, Melinda."

Sarah suddenly understood. "So you've come here to kill us in order to lure Conrad away from the motel." Sarah said.

"Snyder has to die," Mickey countered darkly. "Listen, please. I don't want to hurt anyone, but you have to understand. I was hoping Conrad would finish Snyder off for me; he was always short-tempered and quick to throw the first punch. I thought if Snyder showed up armed, then Conrad would lay him out on the ground."

"Why didn't you just kill that sewer rat yourself?" Amanda asked. "You're pretty good at getting your hands dirty."

"Snyder is connected to some powerful men. I couldn't have his blood on my hands," Mickey explained. "Right now, McCallister's daughter thinks I'm dead. Only Snyder knows I'm alive. He's the last loose end to tie up. Until...Conrad...man, I didn't know he'd take this case so personally."

"That's what friends do when they care about each other," Sarah countered. "Conrad cares about you and came here to serve justice on your behalf. But now you just want Conrad to do your dirty work for you and take the fall for Snyder's murder." Sarah seethed, her mind racing.

"Are we going to kill them or what?" Melinda interrupted impatiently. "Mickey, Macey is waiting for us and you still have to kill Snyder. And we both know that by now that man's thugs are probably wondering where their boss is."

"I know, I know," Mickey said as he shook his head. "But not here in front of the windows." Regretfully, he aimed his gun at Sarah again. "Okay, ladies, into the kitchen," he said in a grim but sorrowful voice.

Ali began to cry. Amanda reached out and took her hand. Sarah steadied herself and looked past Mickey toward the last of the daylight outside. She saw the rain finally transform into pure, white snow.

CHAPTER SEVEN

Sarah studied the inside of the coffee shop's walk-in refrigerator as she rubbed her arms. "I knew it. I didn't think Mickey would have the guts to kill us yet," she said.

"Yeah, he's a real nice guy," Amanda said sarcastically. "Los Angeles, remind me to stick a sock in my mouth the next time I feel a bit adventurous."

"Don't give up yet," Sarah reassured her. "We're still alive. Ali, how are you doing, honey?"

Ali stood at the back of the cooler, rubbing her cold arms with her hands. "I'm alive...that's good."

"Yes, it is," Sarah said, offering Ali a supportive smile. "Honey, we're going to get out of this. Don't you worry."

Ali nodded her head as her teeth began to chatter. She

looked around at the boxes of pastries stacked on the metal shelves. She didn't mind being locked in the refrigerator after the terrifying experience of being forced out of the kitchen at gunpoint. "My mom is going to be so mad," she moaned in misery.

"Maybe not," Sarah said. Her mind was racing as she evaluated their situation. Even though Mickey had been smart enough to disarm her, he had not been smart enough to check the heavily insulated cooler for anything that might be helpful. "Amanda, I need your help," she said, pointing at the metal shelves.

"Okay, MacGyver," Amanda said excitedly, despite the chill, "what do you have in mind? Are you going to make a bomb out of a toilet paper roll?"

"No. But," Sarah said in a hopeful voice, "maybe we can make some noise. Mickey and his wife took off, but Ali's mother is sure to come by sooner or later. We need to let her know we're trapped in here."

"Hey, that's right," Amanda said. She felt herself begin to fill with hope and looked at Ali. "Will your mother be coming by to check on you?"

"My mother always comes by after closing to do the books," Ali said and checked the pink watch wrapped around her left wrist. "So about ten minutes from now my life will be officially over."

"Be brave," Sarah said, focusing on the task ahead. She

began moving boxes off the top of the metal shelf beside her. Amanda and Ali took the boxes and set them down. When the shelf was clear, Sarah began working on removing a single metal bar with her numb hands. The task was tedious and finally Amanda had to lend an extra pair of hands to leverage a single bar loose. It finally came free in her hands.

"Okay," Sarah said, breathing hard, "let's start tapping out an SOS."

Amanda and Ali watched as Sarah began striking the inside of the cooler door. They covered their ears against the noise and waited. Twenty long minutes passed. Just when Sarah was about to give up and start formulating a new plan, the cooler door was yanked open and a short, plump woman with a scared face appeared. "Ali's not at fault here. We'll explain later," Sarah told the startled woman, and then grabbed Amanda's hand. "Ali, we'll be back!" she promised as they raced out of the cooler.

Ali's mother stared at her daughter. "Young lady?" she asked. Ali sighed.

Sarah raced into the coffee shop and grabbed her coat. "I hope we're not too late," she said, throwing on her coat.

Amanda slid her own coat on and ran for the door. "Mickey wouldn't kill Conrad, would he?" she asked.

"Maybe not Mickey, but his wife sure will," Sarah said. She dashed outside into the heavily falling snow. The street was now completely white. Not a single vehicle was moving. The only sign of movement that caught her eye were Snyder's two men, who were walking down the sidewalk toward Sarah and Amanda. Sarah froze. "Don't move," she warned, wishing she still had her gun.

Amanda turned to see the thugs approaching. Both men were armed. "I'm not moving an inch," she replied as snowflakes settled in her hair.

"Where is Mr. Smith?" one of the men asked Sarah when they were close enough. His voice held no compassion or mercy.

"Where were you?" Sarah retorted, thinking fast. "I thought you were supposed to be watching us. Where were you when those armed criminals locked us in the cooler of that coffee shop?"

The men looked at each other in confusion. "Who?"

"Two men who said Snyder sent them to replace you," Sarah said in a convincingly upset voice. "They locked me and my friend in the cooler and told us they would be back later to kill us. The owner of the coffee shop just showed up and let us out. Now, I want answers and I want them now!"

"Yeah," Amanda added, hoping she sounded tough.

The thugs were silent. The quiet of the cold snowy night

closed in around them. "Snyder has been acting funny," one of them finally said quietly to the other.

"He could be planning to go black," the second man muttered.

"Go black?" Sarah asked.

"Kill off his zone, leave it black, and relocate without leaving a trace."

"So that's why those two men said they were here to replace you," Sarah said, finding confidence in her attempt to deceive Snyder's minions. Perhaps, she prayed, she could scare them away without a single shot being fired.

Amanda had caught on to Sarah's plan and now she jumped on board. "At first we thought it was you two goons who were locking us in the cooler. You all look the same...same haircut, same face, same mean eyes. You boys don't date much, do you?"

As if they were twins who could reach each other's minds, the two men lowered their guns in unison. "Snyder is going black," the first man said, tucking his gun away into a shoulder holster. "He's been incommunicado long enough. He'll be after us, next."

"Let's go," the second man agreed. He pointed a threatening finger at Sarah and Amanda. "You never saw us. If you say otherwise, Snyder or no Snyder, we'll make you regret every single syllable."

Sarah raised her hands into the air. "All I want to do is get out of this town, guys. I didn't come here to die."

"Let's keep it that way," the first man warned, and the two of them turned and sprinted away.

Sarah waited until they had vanished into the snow before speaking. "Let's go," she told Amanda quickly.

Amanda grabbed Sarah and hugged her. "You, love, are a genius, and my hero."

"Experience and nothing else," Sarah dismissed the praise with a sigh and then hugged her friend back. "I took a dangerous chance that paid off."

Amanda patted Sarah's shoulder. "You mean you used your brain and it paid off."

"Let's hope so." Sarah hurried around to the driver's side door of the SUV. The falling snow felt different from the snow in Alaska. Even though it was clean and white, it wasn't *her* snow; it wasn't the same snow that covered her cabin and transformed her remote world into something strange and wonderful.

"Are you okay, Los Angeles?" Amanda asked, pausing as she opened the passenger's side door.

"Huh? Oh, I'm fine." Sarah focused her mind. She could

think only of Conrad. She hurried to climb into the driver's side seat and buckled her seat belt. "This snowstorm isn't going to help anyone."

"We've been through worse," Amanda reminded her. She pointed at the road. "Floor it, love. We have to get back to that roach motel before the fat lady sings."

Sarah rolled her eyes. Only Amanda could twist American sayings like that. "Hold on to your seat," she said as the SUV roared off through the snow.

CHAPTER EIGHT

*A*t the motel, Conrad groaned in pain as his eyes fluttered open. "You're awake," he heard Snyder say in a sour voice.

"What..." Conrad could see only blurry images before his eyes and he was in pain. An awful smell emanated from the dirty carpet his face was pressed against. The foul odor was a mixture of old cigarette smoke, rotten food and sickly-sweet liquor that nearly made Conrad vomit.

"Your friend Mickey decided to pay you a visit, remember?" Snyder asked bitterly. Conrad blinked blearily and looked up to see Snyder on a rickety wooden chair with his arms tied behind his back and his ankles tied to the legs of the chair, powerless to assist Conrad. Not that he would have offered to help if the situation had permitted him to do so anyway. "He's coming back to kill us."

Conrad lifted his face off the floor and tried to move but found that the pain was coming from his hands that were tied behind his back and his ankles that were tied together. "Messings?" he called out.

He looked around the room as best he could from his position until he spotted the chief lying unconscious on the bed in the middle of the motel room. "Messings is alive," Snyder assured Conrad in a tired voice. "Listen to me. We need to work as a team. If you help me, I'll forget about our little encounter and even let Messings live out the remainder of his miserable life."

Conrad struggled to keep his nose away from the carpet. He waited until his mind focused and his vision cleared. He vaguely remembered Mickey's sudden, violent arrival. The shock and anguish of seeing him alive was almost as terrible as the blow he had landed on Conrad's jaw to knock him out. He took another breath before speaking. "I heard Mickey say...you had to die."

"Yes," Snyder confirmed. "Detective Spencer, your friend intends to kill me because he discovered I knew he was alive. The man who I cremated was only a bum. I took an X-ray before the cremation and ran a private dental check to confirm my suspicions. Mickey fooled me and paid off Hank Dean to support his plan. It seems like Mr. Dean was playing both sides but ended up taking a hard nose dive."

Just then, Chief Messings moaned in pain from the bed.

Mickey had struck hard, swift, and fast. "How could he betray me?" Conrad whispered to himself as sorrow and fury erupted anew in his heart. "Mickey...how...why? He was my friend."

"The only friend you have in this life is yourself, Detective Spencer," Snyder pointed out in a tired, bitter voice. "Now, if you assist me, we can walk out of this alive and part peacefully. Can we agree to work as a team?"

"Drop dead," Conrad snapped. "I wouldn't help you if my life depended on it. You're a filthy worm, Snyder. You may wear a fancy suit and talk with clever words and fool all the people in your nice little town, but underneath it all, where it counts, you're nothing more than a filthy worm that ought to be stepped on."

"Very well," Snyder replied quietly, "choose your own path."

Conrad fell silent. He tested the strength of his bonds and clenched his jaw in frustration to find the knots solid and unmoving.

Moments later, the door to the motel room opened and Mickey walked in with his wife. With a look of regret in his eyes, he closed the door and gazed down at his former friend. "Conrad—"

"Don't talk to me," Conrad growled fiercely. Breathing hard, he gritted out, "You were my friend, Mickey...my friend, man, and you betrayed me."

"No," Mickey begged, dropping down to his knees. "Conrad, you have to believe me, I never intended for us to be at odds like this. I called you for help...I..."

"Untie me and let me help you now, then," Conrad countered. "If you really are my friend, untie me right now."

"No," Melinda said quickly. "Mickey, my sister will be here any minute with Macey. We have to end this."

Mickey stared at Conrad in remorse. "Your friend called a payphone. It was our signal...My wife thought it was her sister and answered the call. I...we...caught up with your friends at a coffee shop in town. I didn't kill them," he added hastily, seeing the furious, fearful look in Conrad's eyes. "I just locked them in a walk-in cooler. I'm not going to kill anyone but Snyder," he promised.

"What?" Melinda asked in a shocked voice. "Mickey, are you crazy? We can't leave any witnesses. Think about your daughter, for crying out loud."

"I am thinking about Macey," Mickey snapped at his wife. "Melinda, I'm not going to kill the only real friend I ever had. Conrad and I have history. We...made it through some real tough times together."

"My sister is risking her life watching Macey and driving here to pick us up," Melinda yelled. "Mickey, you'd better do your part."

Mickey stood up. "Only Snyder dies," he told her firmly. "Melinda, I mean it. Conrad and I are solid...I owe him, okay?"

"What do you owe that man, then?" Melinda cried hysterically, pointing her gun at Chief Messings. "Is he more important than our own daughter?"

"No," Mickey said. He leaned back against the door. "But I can't look my daughter in her sweet eyes knowing that I've killed two more innocent men, Melinda. This has to end here. Snyder will die, and only Snyder."

"And that's your final answer?" Melinda asked in a suddenly calm, low voice that sent alarm through Conrad's chest.

"Yes." Mickey was at the door, looking down at the gun in his hands.

Conrad watched as Melinda slowly raised her gun and turned around to face her husband. "Oh, Mickey, I wish you hadn't said that."

Mickey stared at his wife. "Melinda, what are you doing?"

"She's betraying you," Snyder laughed. "Oh, this is very amusing. At least I'll get a good show before I die."

Melinda ignored Snyder. Her eyes were laser-focused on Mickey's face. "My sister isn't coming to pick me up.

McCallister's daughter is. She's had Macey this whole time."

"What?" Mickey asked, reeling back as if from a physical blow.

"Oh, come on, Mickey," Melinda snapped, "did you really think I forgave you for putting my daughter's life at risk? Carly McCallister came to me, not you. She came to me and gave me a choice...you or my daughter. That's why I gave Dean the number to the payphone. He was supposed to give the number to Carly. But when you decided to kill Dean, I couldn't let you find the number, so I put the number in a trash bag and shoved it into the oven hoping to cause a fire."

"You..." Mickey said in shock.

"I was going to kill Carly McCallister for you, Mickey...I really wanted to forgive you and believe that you were putting your family first. I had it all planned out. But now I see that you will never put me or Macey first." Melinda's eyes were wide with wrath.

"But—"

"But what?" Melinda screamed, on the verge of tears. "You created a brilliant plan to fool Carly McCallister and kill Snyder," she said, her voice suddenly changing from angry to loving, "but then...oh, Mickey, your old friend showed up and you...I saw you start to change." Her voice became furious again. "Your plan with Dean failed. Conrad showed up but he didn't kill Snyder like you hoped he would, and here we are, one big messed up family with more loose ends than we can handle, all because you can't step up. Not even for your wife. Not even for your own beloved daughter." Melinda blinked once and tears ran down her cheeks, but she stood steadily. "Well it ends now!"

Mickey stared at his wife and then looked down at Conrad. "I couldn't kill you," he told Conrad in a pained voice. "We go way back...we bled together, you and me. I...when you showed up here, Conrad, everything changed. I didn't know what to do. My brain tried to work you into the problem, but..."

"I get it, okay?" Conrad cut Mickey off and looked up at Melinda. "Finish the job, sister," he told her. "If you're going to shoot me, do it. Enough with the talk."

Just then, Chief Messings let out another moan, turned over on his side and rolled off the bed. He hit the ground hard, landing out of sight. Melinda gritted her teeth in frustration at the delay. "Put that man back on the bed," she ordered Mickey, gesturing with the gun.

Mickey put his hands out in front of him. "Easy now," he said nervously. "Melinda, don't do anything that you'll regret. We have Macey to think about."

"Do it now!" Melinda screamed.

"Okay, okay!" Mickey ran over to Chief Messings and

knelt down. As he did so, Chief Messings opened his eyes a fraction and nodded toward his ankle. "My gun," he whispered, and then let out another moan.

Mickey licked his lips. With his back to Melinda, he knew she couldn't see his hands. Making a split-second decision, he reached towards Chief Messings' right ankle and retrieved the gun sitting in the holster. He left the gun on the floor at his feet, making it look like part of his struggle to haul Chief Messings' limp body back onto the bed.

"There," he told Melinda from the far side of the dingy motel bed, breathing hard, when he finally accomplished it. "Now, please, calm down and let's talk."

Snyder laughed quietly. "Oh, this is quite amusing," he said. "To die in a comedy act."

"Shut up!" Melinda yelled, but she was still focused on her husband. She couldn't see that Snyder was slowly attempting to free his wrist behind his back, as Conrad watched quietly from the floor. He had to admire Snyder's dogged struggle. The man must be in some pain, as Conrad could see his skin straining against the rope and the handcuffs. He seemed to be working to free only one hand—Conrad realized the man probably had a cell phone in his jacket pocket that he was planning to dial surreptitiously.

"This is all your fault, Mickey," Melinda was still ranting.

"You want to talk? No, you're going to listen. You destroyed our family with your gambling. At first, you told me you were only betting on a few basketball games...no harm, just for fun. But then our bank account started to run out...and then our savings vanished. I didn't even have money to buy Macey a pair of shoes for the new school year!"

"I know, I know," Mickey said, lowering his eyes in shame. "You have to understand. I kept thinking that I could get back all the money I lost, I could make it all go away, if I just hit it big on one game. But I kept losing...and losing..."

"And losing," Melinda added fiercely. "And now, Mickey, you've lost the most important thing in your life: your daughter. I will never let Macey love you ever again, do you hear me?"

Mickey bowed his head. He looked down at Chief Messings' gun lying at his feet. His heart was sick at the choice he had to make: either let his wife kill his best friend and turn his daughter against him, or swallow his pride and take an even bigger risk. "One last game," he whispered, so that even Conrad could barely hear him, and then he grabbed his chest.

"What is it?" Melinda asked.

"My...chest," Mickey said in a horribly strained voice, and then he dropped to the floor.

Melinda froze for an instant in shock. "Oh Mickey, I can't believe I was going to—we've been through so much pain —" She raced frantically to her husband. "Mickey, don't—"

Melinda stopped short.

Mickey was pointing Chief Messings' gun at her. "Put down the gun, baby," he said in a heartbroken voice.

Melinda dropped the gun abruptly onto the dirty carpet. Her face contorted in a mixture of rage and betrayal. "You...I hate you!" she said in a hollow voice, and a flood of fierce tears began to roll down her cheeks.

Mickey stood up and wrapped his arms around his wife. "We're going to be okay," he promised her. "Somehow, you, me and Macey, we're going to be okay. We can't run anymore, and we can't hide, but the truth will set us free."

Melinda struggled against Mickey's embrace but finally collapsed into his arms, softening in sobs of despair instead of anger. "How, Mickey? We have no money...no home...nothing..."

At that moment, Snyder finally freed his wrist. He inched his hand toward his coat pocket—not knowing that Conrad was watching him. Just before Snyder reached into his pocket, Conrad shot out his tied-together feet and kicked the leg of the decrepit chair Snyder was sitting on. The leg gave way, and Snyder crashed down onto the carpet.

As everyone turned to look at Snyder, the door to the room suddenly burst open and two armed men stormed in. A tall, thin woman in an elegant, long jacket walked in behind the two men. "Ah, Mickey," she said in a disgusted voice. She began brushing snow off her short black hair.

Mickey turned and stared into the cold, gray eyes of Carly McCallister. He swallowed in fear. "Hello, Carly. Where's my daughter?"

"In the limousine," Carly replied coolly. She motioned at the two armed men. "Take the lovebirds outside. We're going to take a ride."

"No, please—Carly, you promised—" Melinda begged.

Snyder, from his awkward position on the floor, laughed quietly and cruelly at this. Conrad wished he could still reach him to kick him in response.

But Conrad looked up and saw one more thing. Mickey, with his hands still wrapped around Melinda's shoulders, was still holding Chief Messings' gun, hidden from Carly's view.

Conrad read Mickey's eyes. He knew. "No," he mouthed urgently.

"What choice do I have, old friend?" Mickey whispered back. Then he said aloud, "I didn't really want to kill

Hank Dean. He threatened to go to Snyder if I didn't give him more money. I'm sorry, Conrad...I really am."

"Don't," Conrad begged.

Mickey closed his eyes and whispered in his wife's ear. "I'm so sorry...forgive me...I love you." Conrad watched, helpless, from his position on the floor.

Mickey drew in a deep breath, but before he could make another move, Sarah appeared in the doorway and yelled, "Freeze!" Conrad was momentarily surprised to see her pointing a shotgun at Carly, but realized she must have found it in Chief Messings' patrol car. "Drop your guns, now!"

"Yeah, drop your guns," Amanda ordered, appearing in the doorway brandishing a broom. Conrad almost laughed at the absurdity of this, until he watched her swing the broom handle in a low, vicious arc, surprising Carly's two thugs with a swift crack at their shins. As they yelped and doubled over in pain, Amanda stood tall and held her broomstick primly. "We've got you surrounded."

Carly's men dropped their guns and slowly raised their hands into the air.

But it wasn't enough. Conrad watched his old friend, whose face was still frozen in a mask of sadness and anger.

"No," Mickey whispered, "she has to die." He pushed Melinda out of his arms and spun around. With tense hands, he aimed his gun at Carly and prepared to fire. Carly threw her hands up as if she could protect her face and screamed.

Click...click...

Sarah breathed a sigh of relief. The gun was empty. She heard Chief Messings mumble a quick apology to Mickey. "I guess I forgot to load the gun."

"No!" Mickey yelled, tossing the gun aside. "That woman has my daughter."

"Oh, no she doesn't," Amanda smiled and looked behind her. "Sweetheart, come here."

A precious little girl in a white coat, her eyes wide with fear, appeared next to Amanda. "Mommy...Daddy?"

"My baby," Melinda cried out and ran to her daughter. Mickey followed.

"Hey, untie me," Conrad called out to Sarah.

Amanda laughed. "I'll handle him, you handle the thugs," Amanda told Sarah and hurried over to Conrad. Sarah kept the two thugs covered with the shotgun while she watched Amanda out of the corner of her eye.

When Amanda finished untying the knots, Conrad stood up, rubbing his wrists. He walked over to stand next to

Sarah. Cautiously, he studied the two men standing in front of him with their arms still raised in the air. "Sarah, I want nothing more than to turn them in, but I don't even know who we can trust here in this state. You heard what the chief was saying about that earlier." Sarah nodded. She had reluctantly come to the same conclusion as Conrad.

"It's over," Conrad told the two men as he scooped up their guns. "Take that woman and get lost."

Carly looked daggers at Conrad at this, but turned to lock eyes with Mickey. "This isn't over," she hissed. "You can run, Mickey Slate, but I'll find you."

"Get lost," Conrad snapped at Carly in a voice that sent chills through her. "And lady, trust me, if anything ever happens to Mickey or his family, I'll come looking for you personally. I'll make it my life's mission to track you down. I have contacts in the FBI, the CIA, and the NSA as well as overseas. You'll be the one who won't be able to hide from me. It won't matter if you run to Russia, China or even North Korea. I'll find you." Conrad stared Carly down, his gaze livid with vitriol for what she had done to his friend.

Sarah knew if she had been the target of that look, she would have been nearly crippled. Watching the fear on Carly's face, Sarah knew that this red-haired woman knew—in her heart—that if she dared attempt to harm Mickey Slate and his family again, then she would certainly become a hunted woman. "You're not worth it," she spat futilely at Mickey and walked out into the snowy night.

"Go," Conrad told the two men. Cowed by his dismissive tone, the two men followed Carly out into the snow and vanished into the night.

"What now?" Mickey asked Conrad as he pulled his daughter lovingly into his arms.

"You go to jail for murder," Conrad said sadly. "Mickey, you have five minutes with your family and then...I'm placing you under arrest for the murder of Hank Dean."

Snyder began to snicker from his chair where it had collapsed onto the floor. But then, he made a strange, half-strangled sound. "Help...I can't breathe...my chest..." he said in a panicked voice.

Sarah turned and with a sinking feeling, she knew Snyder wasn't acting. She ran over to the man just as he lost consciousness. Hastily handing the shotgun to Conrad, she checked for a pulse and then for breathing and then rapidly untied him as she cried out, "Amanda, help me. We need to do CPR. I'll breathe for him, you pump. Conrad, get an ambulance out here."

"Why?" Melinda cried. "Let that awful man die."

"Because we're cops," Sarah explained grimly, getting

into position, "and cops seek justice through the law. Not through luck."

Amanda ran to Sarah's side, dropped to her knees and positioned herself. "Ready?"

"Start pumping." Sarah leaned down to breathe life into Snyder.

Conrad was already on the phone calling for an ambulance. As soon as he hung up, he swiftly untied Chief Messings and helped him sit up. Then he went to stand next to his old friend and patted his shoulder.

In the quiet of the dingy motel room, Mickey and Melinda clutched their young daughter, and everyone watched as Sarah and Amanda worked to save the life of an evil man.

Sarah sat wearily in the rental SUV in the parking lot an hour later, watching as the dead body of Snyder Smith was rolled out of the room on a stretcher. She closed her eyes briefly. It had all happened so swiftly.

While she and Amanda had given brief statements to the paramedics, and then to another cop from the local police department, Mickey Slate had been arrested for the murder of Hank Dean. Sarah had watched Conrad's stiff posture as Chief Messings drove

Mickey's wife and daughter back into town in his patrol car.

The ambulance finally pulled out of the parking lot. In all her years on the force, she never got used to the feeling of seeing an ambulance leaving a crime scene with no lights or sirens. It meant that something was over. It meant that some things cannot be undone.

Sarah climbed out of the SUV and approached Conrad where he stood at the far end of the parking lot, staring into the dark, snowy line of trees just past the motel building.

"Are you okay?" she asked him gently.

Conrad wiped at a tear as snowflakes settled in his hair. "No," he said brokenly. "I had to put handcuffs on my friend, Sarah. I had to see his little girl cry out for her daddy and his wife crumble. And for what? A stupid gambling bet?"

Sarah watched Conrad wipe his tears, her heart aching for him. "I'm so sorry."

"So am I." Conrad turned away from the trees to look into Sarah's sincere, beautiful eyes. "Thanks for being there when I needed you," he said. Leaning forward, he kissed Sarah on her forehead. "You're something special."

Sarah felt a warm sense of peace and security surrounding her when she felt the touch of Conrad's lips on her forehead. To her own surprise, she impulsively reached out and wrapped both of her arms around Conrad's right arm. "Let's go home, Conrad. I'm tired of Minnesota." Despite the events of the day, she felt a small smile curling her lips.

Conrad nodded his head and walked Sarah back to the SUV, where Amanda was waiting for them. When Amanda saw Sarah hugging Conrad's arm, she smiled to herself, crawled into the backseat, and buckled up. "Time to go home," she announced happily.

CHAPTER NINE

*T*wo weeks later, Conrad knocked on the back door to Sarah's cabin. Sarah answered the door wearing a fuzzy pink robe. "Kinda early, isn't it?" she asked him with a puzzled look.

"Yeah, kinda early, isn't it?" Amanda echoed cheerfully from her seat at the kitchen table, where Conrad could see she too was wearing a robe, in a lighter shade of pink. Conrad looked again at Sarah and then looked past her at Amanda. Both women had their hair tied into tight buns and their faces covered with some kind of strange mud. "I...brought coffee and muffins," he said and smiled nervously.

"Oh, just let him in," Amanda told Sarah, "and close the door. You're letting out all the good heat."

Sarah leaned her head outside and looked up at the low, dark gray clouds. A storm was on its way. "Come in," she told Conrad.

Conrad stepped inside, kicked the snow off his boots, and followed Sarah over to the kitchen table carrying a bag of chocolate muffins and a cardboard drink holder containing three tall cups of coffee. "I talked with Mickey's wife last night," he said, sitting down.

"Coffee and muffins first," Amanda ordered.

"Yes, Miss Creature from the Black Lagoon," Conrad teased.

"Not funny," Amanda said, but she grinned despite herself.

Conrad looked up at Sarah. Even though Sarah's face was covered with what appeared to be mud, her amazing beauty shined bright to him. "Coffee?"

"Sure," Sarah smiled behind her masque and sat down next to him. "So, what did Melinda have to say?"

"Well," Conrad began, doling out the coffee cups, "Macey has been placed in the custody of her aunt for the time being. Melinda has been ordered by the courts to get counseling and perform a whole bunch of community service. But I think she's going to be okay. Mickey's testimony that he forced Melinda to help him is really what kept her out of a prison cell."

Sarah took her cup of coffee from Conrad and removed the lid, inhaling its fragrant aroma. "What about Mickey?"

Conrad sighed. "Mickey will spend the rest of his life in prison," he replied.

"I'm sorry," Sarah said, placing her hand over Conrad's comfortingly.

"Me, too," Amanda agreed somberly. "But...I have to say, it's hard to stay sad with these muffins," she added with a small smile.

Conrad nodded and forced a smile to his face at Amanda's joke. "On a more positive note," he said, "Chief Messings will be arriving in town in three days to begin his new job here in Snow Falls."

Amanda rolled her eyes. "Let's just hope he gets along with the grizzly bears. Who knows, maybe the grizzly bears will think he's one of them?"

"Stop it," Sarah laughed. "Chief Messings is a good man. I think he's going to fit in well."

"And take up a whole lot of sidewalk," Amanda grinned. "Okay, no more fat jokes. I promise. I think Chief Messings and his wife are going to be upstanding citizens of our fine community...and give the diner a whole lot of business."

Conrad rolled his eyes. "You're hopeless." He turned to Sarah. "How's your book coming?"

"I still have writer's block," she answered miserably.

"You'll get there. I know you will," Conrad comforted her and sipped his coffee. "Anyway, I have today off. I figured I could help you ladies at the coffee shop a while."

Sarah looked into Conrad's eyes. She saw a hurt and lonely man who, at this moment, needed a friend more than he needed romance. She wanted nothing more than to be there for him. Swallowing down her own budding feelings for him, she smiled cheerfully. "I have a lot of renovation work to do. You might regret the offer."

"I doubt it," Conrad grinned. He looked at Amanda. "Hurry up and eat, Swamp Thing," he teased.

Amanda stuck her tongue out at him and polished off her muffin in one bite.

Sarah smiled and took a sip of her coffee. Outside, the winds began to howl through the trees as the storm picked up. Another case was behind her and she was back home in her cabin, safe and sound. Life was good.

Or was it?

Far away, a shadowy figure walked down the street

leading to Sarah's old neighborhood in Los Angeles, stopped in front of a quaint two-story home, and grinned under the clear blue California sky. "Oh, Sarah, let the games begin," the figure whispered in a gleeful voice. "Let the games begin and the snowmen be built, Sarah. Oh yes, my love, the snowmen will write the first chapter for us and after that, we'll go where the snow takes us."

ABOUT THE AUTHOR

Wendy Meadows is an emerging author of cozy mysteries. She lives in "The Granite State" with her husband, two sons, two cats and lovable Labradoodle.

When she isn't working on her stories she likes to tend to her flowers, relax with her pets and play video games with her family.

Get in Touch with Wendy
www.wendymeadows.com

amazon.com/author/wendymeadows

goodreads.com/wendymeadows

bookbub.com/authors/wendy-meadows

facebook.com/AuthorWendyMeadows

twitter.com/wmeadowscozy

Made in the USA
Middletown, DE
06 September 2021

47723087R00082